I AM CANADA

SINK AND DESTROY

The Battle of the Atlantic

by Edward Kay

Scholastic Canada Ltd.
Toronto New York London Auckland Sydney
Mexico City New Delhi Hong Kong Buenos Aires

While the events described and some of the characters in this book may be based on actual historical events and real people, Bill O'Connell is a fictional character created by the author, and his story is a work of fiction.

A Dear Canada Book. Published by Scholastic Canada Ltd.
SCHOLASTIC and I AM CANADA and logos are trademarks and/or registered trademarks of Scholastic Inc.

www.scholastic.ca

Library and Archives Canada Cataloguing in Publication

Kay, Edward, author
Sink and destroy : the battle of the Atlantic / Edward Kay.

(I am Canada)
Issued in print and electronic formats.
ISBN 978-1-4431-0781-5 (bound).--ISBN 978-1-4431-2884-1 (html)
1. World War, 1939-1945--Campaigns--Atlantic Ocean--Juvenile fiction. I. Title. II. Series: I am Canada
PS8621.A79S56 2014 jC813'.6 C2014-901807-X
C2014-901808-8

6 5 4 3 2 1 Printed in Canada 114 14 15 16 17 18

The display type was set in Rosewood.
The text was set in Minion.

First printing September 2014

For the veterans who shared their stories with me, especially John Schumacher, RCN.

Prologue

"Incoming torpedoes!" shouted the ASDIC operator. "Sounds like a freight train! They're coming straight at us from the stern, off to port side!"

Without a moment's hesitation the captain called out, "Hard to starboard!"

The bow swung round and the ship leaned over at a crazy angle. I hung on to my 4-inch gun to keep from getting thrown overboard. From my position I could see two trails of bubbles racing toward us from out of the dark, frigid water. Beyond that, there was just the blackness of a North Atlantic night.

After months of preparing and waiting, I finally had my first encounter with a U-boat. And now, as I watched the torpedo trails homing in on us and felt the ship turning agonizingly slowly as the helmsman threw the wheel around, I wondered if it would be my last.

I thought back to how this had started. It seemed so far away, almost another lifetime.

Chapter One
Iroquois, Ontario, September 10, 1939

The first thing I felt was a gentle tug on the end of the fishing rod, so light that you could almost mistake it for the lure being drawn along by the current. But my dad had trained me to do this since I was eight years old, so I knew exactly what it meant.

I opened my eyes, almost reluctantly, despite knowing there was a fish nibbling at my lure. I had been enjoying the warm, late-summer sun on my face, the gentle rocking of the rowboat on the waves. But now all my senses were focused on that fishing line. I tried not to move, tried not to breathe. This was where you could lose the contest before it even started. If the fish sensed any unnatural motion, it would get spooked, let go of the bait and bolt away. But if you waited too long to make your move, it would nibble the bait right off your hook, then leave you in the middle of the river, minus one fish, feeling like an idiot.

It was the first weekend after Labour Day. The summer vacationers, most of them from the

American side of the river, had gone home and wouldn't be back again until school was out next June. So the St. Lawrence was quiet. It was one of my favourite times of the year. No mosquitoes or deer flies to annoy me, no powerboats and water skiers scaring the fish away. Nothing to disturb me. Just the golden September light shimmering across the wavetops. But I knew that it couldn't stay this way for long. In just a couple of weeks there would be a chill in the morning air and the leaves on the maple and oak trees along the riverbank would turn to a blaze of colour. Icy winter winds would close in soon after that, then the river would freeze over completely and there'd be no more afternoons on the boat until the ice thawed the next spring.

But right now that was far from my thoughts. The pole bent slightly as the fish at last took the bait. I gave the rod a short, sharp tug upward, the way Dad had taught me, to set the hook firmly into the fish's mouth. An instant later the line jerked hard as the fish dove, trying to escape.

"Looks like a big one, Billy!" my brother George whispered to me.

I let out some line. I always did that at the beginning of a fight. If you didn't give a big fish like this some play, it could easily snap your line and get away. I knew I had to be patient and let it gradually wear itself out. Whenever I felt the line go limp, I reeled in the slack. When the fish began to tug again, I released a bit of line. When there were only a few yards of line left, I saw a dark green shadow down in the water off the left side of the rowboat — a big bass. They were a smart fish with a lot of fight. Sometimes when a bass got this close, and catching it seemed like a sure thing, it would summon its remaining strength and make a run straight at your broadside, just like a torpedo. At the last possible moment, it would dive under you and out the other side, so your line would get snagged under the keel and snap. Then you'd have nothing to show for your efforts but a lost lure and a story about a big bass that outsmarted you. And that's just what this one started to do.

I called to George, "It's heading straight for us! Get ready with the landing net."

George scrambled to the side, using his strong arm muscles to compensate for his polio-withered legs. He moved fast.

As the fish shot toward our boat, I drew the rod away and led it around the bow so the line wouldn't get snagged. George reached over the side and plunged the landing net in, all the way to his elbow. Then he whipped the net upward. There was an explosion of sun-fractured water. A moment later the big bass was flopping around in the bottom of our boat.

I felt a rush of triumph. And it wasn't just the thrill of the hunt. The Great Depression had hit my town hard, and my family with it. My father had spent half of the past ten years unemployed or doing menial jobs like chopping wood and shovelling snow to pay the bills. My three brothers and my sister and I needed to be fed, so every fish we caught, we ate. It was never just for sport. It was survival. Whenever I came home with a good catch, I knew that I'd see a look of happiness and relief on my mother's face. Counting the fish I'd just caught, George and I now had two large bass and a pickerel.

"Well, that's a good haul for one day," he said. "Let's head home." We didn't have an outboard motor. We couldn't afford one, or even the gas to run it. George began rowing us back, his big arms propelling the boat forward.

As we rounded a bend, our house came into view on the shoreline. My parents were standing near the dock. I figured Mom would be thrilled to see how many fish we'd caught, so when we got within hailing distance, I shouted, "They're biting!" and held up one of the bass in my right hand and the pickerel in the other. But neither Mom or Dad smiled. Their arms were crossed and they both had a strange sort of heaviness in their expressions. I knew straight away that something really bad had happened.

As George brought us up to the dock, I jumped out, grabbed the bow rope and quickly tied it up to the cleat with a hitch knot. I held the boat steady as George hauled himself out onto the dock.

"What is it, Dad?" I called out. "What's the matter?"

"Prime Minister King was just on the radio," he replied. "We're at war with Germany and Hitler."

An icy sensation shot through me when I heard those words. It was like some horrible nightmare you couldn't wake up from. From the time I was ten years old, I'd heard about Hitler. He'd been around almost as long as that other big nightmare in our lives, the Great Depression. But for most of that time, unlike the Depression, it was possible to ignore Hitler. The only time I saw him was in a movie theatre, in one of the newsreels they showed before the main feature, and my family didn't have enough money to take us to the pictures very often. So I had only seen Hitler in action a few times. That was more than enough though.

The speeches he gave were like nothing I'd ever seen or heard before. We couldn't understand a word he said, because it was all in German. But there was no mistaking his meaning or tone. He didn't talk. He ranted, shouting angrily, while he waved his arms in the air as if he was striking out at something. The crowds that he ranted at ate it up. On a newsreel I saw, Hitler bellowed "*Sieg Heil!*" — German for "*Hail victory!*" The entire mob, a hundred thousand people, responded by shouting "*Heil!*" and they all threw a Nazi salute, a stiff right arm extended on an angle upward.

In another newsreel, I'd seen the Nuremberg rallies — thousands of people in a huge outdoor arena, shouting, marching around holding flaming torches above them, moving together to make the shape of a giant Swastika, the Nazis' symbol. With their torches and their shouting, they reminded me of the angry mob in the movie *Frankenstein*. I could never forget Hitler, any more than I could forget the terrifying image of Frankenstein's monster roaring down at the crowd of peasants from the top of his burning tower.

Most of my friends at school had the same bad feeling about Hitler and the Nazis as I did. We thought something should be done to stop him before he got too powerful. We knew we'd be the ones who'd have to go fight his armies if he wasn't stopped. But Prime Minister Mackenzie King, and the other world leaders like the British prime minister, Neville Chamberlain, and the American president, Franklin Roosevelt, did nothing. They just seemed to hope that Hitler would go away despite all his ranting and his threats.

Now we were seeing Hitler's rants turn to action. Just over a week earlier, his army had invaded Poland. The CBC radio reports told us how German Luftwaffe bombers were blasting Poland's cities into rubble, killing thousands of civilians, using them as bargaining chips to force the Polish government to surrender. Now, unprepared, Canada had been pulled into the conflict.

The timing of the war seemed all the more cruel, because when it started, the Depression had begun to ease up a little. Not as many businesses were closing, and a few new ones were even opening.

Things were looking up for my family too. Every single lake freighter travelling between Montreal and Thunder Bay had to pass through the lock here in Iroquois, where the St. Lawrence River's rapids made it too dangerous for ships to sail through. The government had built those locks, and my father, who'd spent his life fishing on the river and knew its tricky currents better than anybody, was hired to be the lockmaster. It brought in some steady income for my family at last.

Within a few months of starting that job, my father knew the captains of all the ships. A week after school had finished that summer, the captain of one of the freighters, Frank Jameson, told my dad that a deckhand had jumped ship and asked if he knew of anyone who could fill in. Dad suggested me. Captain Jameson was skeptical about hiring a fifteen-year-old. But he was in a bind, so he took a chance. Mom wasn't very happy about me working on the ship. It meant I would be gone for the next two months until school started again. But even with my father's new job, we could use the extra income, and me being on the ship also meant there was one less mouth to feed. I knew I would miss my family, but the thrill of getting out of Iroquois, earning some money and seeing the world was too tempting to resist. I started work aboard the SS *Huronia* that same day.

We sailed west, reaching Lake Ontario the next morning. It was my first time being on open water and it was an amazing feeling — I figured it was what being at sea must be like. Some of the Great Lakes, like Superior, were so huge that when we sailed across them, we didn't see land for days at a time. I felt far away from the world and its troubles.

By the time the summer was over and I had returned to Iroquois and to school, I felt like Marco Polo, a world traveller returning from distant places with exotic names like Toledo, Detroit and Sault Ste. Marie. I'd also saved a bit of money to help my family out, which was a first. I was so caught up in life aboard the *Huronia* that I had almost forgotten about all the trouble building up overseas. Until that Sunday afternoon when I came home from fishing.

A few weeks later we heard that Germany had defeated Poland. From the outset, the war seemed to be one series of blunders after another for the Allies. The Royal Air Force sent planes to attack the German battleship *Admiral Scheer* and scored three direct hits, but the bombs failed to explode. On September 17 the British aircraft carrier HMS *Courageous*, which was critically important for Atlantic convoy patrol, was sunk by a German submarine. Even then our military leaders insisted that U-boats didn't pose a serious threat. That changed, and soon. A month after the *Courageous* was sunk, another U-boat sailed right into the supposedly impenetrable Royal Navy base at Scapa Flow in northern Scotland and sank the battleship *Royal Oak*, sending 833 crewmen to their graves.

It was infuriating to hear about all these failures. Our side just seemed to bumble and fumble at every turn. Then for a while, over the winter of 1939–1940, things seemed to settle down. After that initial flurry of action, there wasn't much military activity. The press started referring to it as the Phoney War.

Mr. Martin, my grade 11 history teacher, told our class one day that, "This lull could mean that diplomats are working behind closed doors, trying to negotiate a settlement. With any luck, the war will be over by the time you go on summer vacation."

My best friend, Jack Byers, leaned over from the next row of desks and whispered to me, "Is he kidding? We'll be lucky if it's over by the time we graduate — from university."

That's how I felt too, although a lot of the adults didn't seem to share our opinion.

People all over town began to hope that maybe Hitler really did have everything he wanted now, and things would get back to normal. But I kept thinking of him ranting in those newsreels like Frankenstein's roaring monster, and had a sick feeling that Hitler had barely begun to get everything he wanted.

With the war going on, it was hard to concentrate

on school. Guys just a couple of years older than me were enlisting in the forces. I was sixteen now, and could legally leave school and work full-time. In late March of 1940 when the ice broke up and the lake freighters resumed operating, I quit school and signed up on the SS *Huronia* again. Mom was really upset that I had dropped out. She never said so, but I know she must have been thinking of all the hardship we had endured because my father didn't have an education. But with the war on, high-paid jobs were suddenly there for the taking, even for grade 11 dropouts. After ten years of being broke and doing without just about everything that we couldn't grow or catch, and the embarrassment of wearing hand-me-down everything with patches and worn spots, the possibility of a paycheque every two weeks and a decent set of clothes was just too tempting.

By the first week of April, I was back out on the *Huronia*, carrying grain that would be sent to England to help feed Allied troops and civilians. At first it made me feel like I was doing my bit for the war effort, but as the reports of U-boat attacks in the Atlantic began to trickle in, I felt less and less like what I was doing mattered. Those German submarines were sinking our merchant ships faster than they could be built, meaning that a lot of the grain we carried out from the Lakehead on the *Huronia* never made it to the people in Britain who needed it. But I tried not to think about that and just get on with my work aboard the ship. Because I was so used to helping my mom cook for our big family, I had started working in the ship's galley, helping prepare meals for the crew of twenty.

Barely a month after I'd started on the *Huronia* again, I was in the kitchen, just about to serve up breakfast, when there was breaking news over the ship's radio. The phony war was no longer phony. Early that morning the Nazis had invaded France, Belgium, the Netherlands and Luxembourg, moving so quickly that by the time we even heard the news, German troops had already advanced deep into those countries.

Over the next week, every radio broadcast reported a fresh defeat for our side. First the Netherlands surrendered, then Belgium. The Allied armies were pushed back to the English Channel, and France was on the verge of collapse. The reports got so consistently grim that at one point, while we were eating dinner and the news came on announcing yet another German victory, Captain Jameson lost his temper.

"O'Connell, will you turn that damned radio off and give us all a break?" he snapped.

"Yes, sir," I replied sheepishly. I jumped out of my chair and quickly shut it off.

From then on we only played music during our meals. I still listened to the news when I could, but only when I was alone in the galley. It was almost always bad news for the Allied side.

By early June the Allied armies had been forced to retreat across the English Channel, leaving their tanks, trucks and artillery behind. Less than three weeks later, the Nazis had defeated France. Germany now had all the resources of Europe at its disposal; Britain none. Any food and weapons that Britain imported from now on would have to come from Canada and the United States, and there was only one way to do that: cross the Atlantic Ocean. That job would get a lot more difficult now too, because the German submarines moved from Germany to bases on the Atlantic coast of France, bringing them hundreds of miles closer to the combat zone and allowing them to stay out on patrol for an extra two weeks at a time. The result was that they sank more Allied merchant ships than ever. The only bright spot was that Neville Chamberlain had resigned as British prime minister and been replaced by Winston Churchill — who reminded me a bit of a bulldog, with the defiant set of his jaw, and his tough, inspiring speeches.

Through the summer I was really starting to doubt whether my work on the *Huronia* was helping the war effort at all. Everything came to a head one Saturday night in October of 1940. We were picking up a load of grain from the terminal in Port Arthur. Captain Jameson had given most of the crew the evening off. A few of us went for a stroll down the main street in search of something fun to do and ended up in a movie theatre. I bought a Coke and some popcorn, a luxury I would never, ever have considered spending my money on just a year ago.

The lights went down and a newsreel came on. I was expecting the usual mixture of news and puff pieces about things like rodeos and baby pageants. But tonight it was mostly war news, and all of it was grim. "A new phase of the war has begun," said the clipped voice of the newsreel announcer, "one that they are calling the Blitz. Luftwaffe planes are bombing London and the other large British cities almost every night, indiscriminately killing men, women and children."

The announcer went on to say that in one of the worst raids, more than four hundred Londoners were killed, most of them civilians. The newsreel showed London ablaze, firefighters silhouetted against a raging inferno. Then it showed the aftermath, the smoking rubble the morning following that raid. One image really stuck with me. In it, smashed buildings filled the streets and a family, including small children, climbed over the remains of what might have been their house the day before. One was a little girl about the same age as my own sister, Marian. They were all just ordinary people, like my parents and siblings. Just people trying to get by.

Later in the newsreel came a story about a convoy that sailed from Sydney, Nova Scotia, with food and raw materials for Britain. The ships were ambushed by a group of U-boats — the announcer said the Germans called it a "wolf pack" — which sank twenty of the thirty-five merchantmen. Wood, iron ore, mine equipment, oil and grain — quite likely grain that the *Huronia* had carried to the docks — had ended up at the bottom of the ocean. The sailors lucky enough to be rescued were covered in oil, shivering from the icy water, their eyes wide in terror and shock. A hot sensation rose inside me and my muscles seemed to tense up all on their own.

Then came almost the worst part — images of Hitler gloating over his latest conquest. What really got me was his smug expression as he posed for the camera, strutting around like a banty rooster while his aircraft bombed women and children into oblivion. It made me so angry I wanted to drive my fist into his face. I was so mad after that, I could barely sit through the movie. Those images of the bombed families, the terrified sailors, the haunted eyes of the survivors . . . I had to do something about it.

When we arrived at Toronto four days later to offload our grain, I finished my shift, then walked straight to the recruiting office at HMCS *York*. I lied about my age and told the recruitment officer I was seventeen, which I knew could get me into the Navy. I either looked old enough, or they were desperate enough, because the recruiter didn't demand any proof. He told me that because of my shipboard experience, they would put me to the front of the line and to expect to report in about two weeks. In the meantime, he said that I should go home, take care of any business I needed to attend to, and wait for the telegram.

I went back to the ship and told Captain Jameson that I had enlisted and that I would probably be called up soon. I thought he might be angry, but instead he just nodded slowly and said, "You're what the Navy needs, all right."

I offered to stay on until I was called up, but he just shook his head. "I can find another fellow to fill in for you, somebody like me who's too old for combat duty. Now you'd better get home and say goodbye to your family. I hate to say it, but I think we're in for a long war. Give my regards to your father."

Captain Jameson told me that if we'd been heading for Montreal, he'd have taken me right to the lock in Iroquois. But he had orders that as soon as the *Huronia* offloaded, it was to immediately sail back up to the Lakehead for another load of grain.

"Now that France is out of the game, we can't keep up with the orders for wheat," he said. "If you can keep those Jerry submarines from feeding it to the the fish, I'll be grateful. And if you can sink a few of the bastards while you're at it, so much the better."

"I'll do my best, sir," I replied.

"I know you will, O'Connell. I know you will. Good luck."

Chapter Two
October 1940

I took the train back to Iroquois to tell my parents. Being the lockmaster, my father knew that my ship wasn't due to come through, and he and my mother wouldn't be expecting me. So I knocked on the door before opening it. "Mom? Dad? It's me, Billy," I called as I entered the house.

My mother appeared in the hallway a moment later.

"Billy, how come you're home? Is something wrong?" she asked.

"Not exactly. But you'd better sit down," I replied.

In the parlour, with the door closed, I told my parents the news. "I've joined the Navy. They're going to be calling me up in a couple of weeks."

My parents both looked shocked. Nobody in my family had ever been in the military before. My father had a heart murmur, so he hadn't served in the First World War. My older brother Don had inherited the same heart defect, so he hadn't even thought about enlisting. And because he'd been stricken with polio, George wasn't able to serve in the military either.

As soon as it sank in, my mom started to cry. No matter how much the government tried to paint a rosy picture, everyone had heard the stories about how unprepared the Royal Canadian Navy was.

She wiped away her tears, and soon her sadness turned to anger. "This is the stupidest thing you've ever done!" she said. "You're *sixteen*! You're not even old enough to join. I'm going to call that recruiting centre and tell them."

"If you do that," I said, trying to sound calm and in control, "I'll just run away and join the Army with a false ID."

Mentioning the Army made her even more upset. More than three hundred thousand Allied troops had been killed or wounded during Hitler's invasion of France and the Low Countries. Given the choice, I guess my mother decided that my skills as a seaman would at least give me a fighting chance, so at last she relented.

Ten days later I received a letter to report to HMCS *York*. There was a morning train from Montreal to Toronto that stopped in Iroquois. My family walked with me the few blocks from our house to the train station. At 12:14 the train arrived, right on time. There was an awkward moment where nobody knew what to say. I guess everyone wanted to be brave, but I knew that I might never see any of them again. My parents and George and Don were aware of that too, though Marian, and especially Burt, being the youngest, seemed to think it was just a big adventure. I was glad they didn't know any better. The train slowed to a stop, and the conductor opened the doors and shouted, "All aboard!"

"Well, I guess this is it," was the only thing I could think of to say to my parents. "I'll write to you as soon as I can." Everyone was so emotional that we didn't speak very much.

My mother kissed me and squeezed my hand. She was trying to smile, but her eyes kept filling with tears. "Be careful, Billy," was all she could say. Then her voice cracked and she let go and turned away so I wouldn't see her cry. She hated anyone ever seeing her cry.

My dad shook my hand firmly and quietly said, "Take care of yourself, son. Write us when you're settled in."

"I will, Dad," I promised.

George balanced himself on his crutches and leaned in close so nobody else could hear. "Whatever you do, don't end up as a stoker. I heard that if your ship gets torpedoed, those guys down in the engine room don't have a chance."

"Don't worry," I answered. "I won't."

Then I climbed aboard. I took a seat and opened the window so I could wave goodbye.

As the train began to move, Burt started galloping along the platform, yelling, "Send me a flag from one of those German submarines after you capture it!"

"You bet," I called back to him, "if there's enough left of it to send to you by the time we're through with it."

He smiled and saluted me proudly. He was so excited, so confident that we would win.

I saluted back, putting on my bravest smile. But inside, I wondered what sort of a world Burt would inherit, wondered what sort of a world any of us would be living in a few years from now. Then in less than a minute we had pulled out of the station, around a bend in the river and past a thick stand of maple trees. Iroquois disappeared from view as neatly as if it had never existed.

The train got into Toronto a few hours later, and I reported directly to HMCS *York*. First I was given a physical examination. Doctors checked us recruits over for any conditions that would make us unsuitable for military service. I passed my physical, then over the next few days, spent a lot of time writing aptitude tests. I surprised myself by doing well on the math exams. I had never been a particularly good student, but it turned out that I had an aptitude for geometry and spatial relations — a fancy way of saying the relative position of three-dimensional objects. I think it was because I had spent so much time hunting ducks and geese, where I had to aim not at where the flying bird was, but where it would be when the bullet caught up to it.

Then, along with a trainload of other recruits, I was sent out to Halifax.

The two-day trip felt even longer thanks to the hard, overcrowded benches of our old coach. The ride was rough, and between being squeezed in among all these other guys, and the vibration, we couldn't really sleep. So I felt a huge sense of relief when the conductor came through the car and announced that we'd be arriving in ten minutes.

As we neared the station on Hollis Street, I got my first glimpse of Halifax Harbour. It was crammed with merchant ships waiting to join convoys. I counted at least thirty of them at anchor, and more by the docks, plus a sleek destroyer bristling with guns.

At the station a few junior officers were on hand to meet us, and after we piled off with our luggage, we marched the 2 miles to the Navy dockyard. It was only when we passed through the gateway and onto the grounds that I understood exactly how unprepared Canada was for war.

The base had the look of a construction site, with crews pouring concrete and sawing lumber and nailing together wooden frames for buildings, while hundreds of recruits getting their physical training ran past them and around them. A petty officer led us into a hall where we were given our kit, but it was incomplete. We were issued boots, socks and underwear, and were measured for our uniforms. But they didn't have any actual uniforms on hand.

That meant that for the first few days we would have to exercise and parade in our "civvies" — literally the clothes we had worn on our backs to get here. Then three hundred of us new guys were led into a hockey rink.

"All *right*!" whispered a sandy-haired recruit standing behind me. "What a way to spend the war, playing hockey!"

Suddenly a loud voice boomed out of the darkness, and a figure in a neatly pressed naval uniform marched to the front of the crowd.

"My name is Chief Petty Officer Lancaster," the man called out. "Welcome to your new home away from home. There are lockers in the middle of the hall. Stow your gear there, then form a line to my right for hammocks and bedding."

As my eyes adjusted to the dim light, I noticed that the rink had a dirt floor.

The same recruit standing beside me whistled with disbelief. "Get a load of this!" he said. "No barracks. We've got to sleep in a hockey rink."

"Yeah," I whispered back to him. "The least they could have done is laid down some ice and given us skates so we could pass the time."

That got a few quiet laughs from the guys standing around us.

The petty officer didn't seem to overhear any of it, but then looked right at me and said, "And for anyone concerned about the lack of skating opportunities, don't worry. By the time we're finished with you each night, you'll be so tired you'll be lucky to get your boots off before you fall asleep."

I put my suitcase into a locker, then fell into line to get my hammock and bedding. I found a spot to hang my hammock where it wasn't too drafty, and that was that. I noticed then that the guy in the next hammock was the one who'd made the crack about the hockey arena. We introduced ourselves. His name was Ken Luke, and he was from Montreal. "Home of the world's greatest hockey team!" he boasted.

"Oh yeah?" I replied. "Did somebody move the Maple Leafs there and not tell me about it?"

He gave me a wry look. "The *Leafs*? You gotta be kidding me."

"When was the last time the Habs made the finals?" I had him there, because even though neither of our teams had won the Stanley Cup in almost ten years, at least Toronto had made the finals the past three years in a row, unlike the Habs. But we couldn't settle the argument, because the New York Rangers had beaten both our teams to win the Cup that year. So instead we talked about our hometowns. I told him about hunting and fishing in Iroquois.

"Wow, living off the land. You're a regular Davy Crockett," he said. "King of the Wild Frontier."

I laughed. I hadn't thought of it that way before, but I guess to a kid from the city, hunting and fishing for your dinner seemed pretty unusual.

"What's it like in Montreal?" I asked.

"Well," he replied, "since shooting the deer and geese on Mount Royal is frowned on, the closest I've got to hunting is being on the school archery team."

Ken told me about growing up in downtown Montreal. With his stories of delicatessens, jazz music and all kinds of neighbourhoods — French, Italian, Jewish, Greek and Chinese — it seemed so colourful compared to Iroquois.

But there were no delis or jazz music in our hockey arena that first night, or any other kind of entertainment, for that matter. So some of the guys played cards, others read. Most just smoked and talked.

Then Petty Officer Lancaster returned and announced it would be lights out in ten minutes. Ken and I made our way to the bathroom. It was big, cold and drafty with a long line of toilets and sinks, and an open shower area. There was already a long lineup. "Hey, O'Connell, get a load of this. You ever had to wait in a line before just to brush your teeth?"

"Are you kidding?" I answered. "I've got three brothers and a sister. There isn't *anything* I haven't waited in line for!"

He laughed. Everybody was in pretty good spirits despite the less than comfortable surroundings.

As we climbed into our strange new beds, Ken and I figured that we would probably be here just for a couple of days, until they got us sorted out and assigned to our various barracks, wherever those were. The officers turned the lights out, and despite the cold and the scratchy wool blanket, and the difficulty of finding a comfortable position in my hammock, I fell asleep in seconds.

* * *

There were no windows in the rink, so we couldn't tell day from night except by the routine. When six a.m. came around, the junior officers woke us by filing in and banging pots with spoons. They gave us half an hour to shower, shave and get dressed. It turned out there wasn't enough hot water, so by the time I'd had my lukewarm shower and then stood in line waiting for the sink, I had to do my shaving with cold water. But I was so excited about starting my first real day of training, I didn't care.

"All right, Ladies," shouted Petty Officer Lancaster. "Time to work up an appetite for breakfast." I was already hungry, but it was clear that would have to wait. They directed us out to the parade ground. It was still dark when we filed out into the chilly late-autumn air. Lancaster was the instructor for my group.

"Mark this day on your calendars," he called out. "Because today is the day that we start turning you into sailors. And this day begins *now*."

For the next hour we did calisthenics: stretching, jumping jacks, push-ups, squats, sit-ups and lunges. I was pretty fit from all the time I'd spent swimming and rowing and hunting in the woods, but by the end of the hour my eyes were stinging from the sweat running down my forehead and my thigh muscles and my shoulders were getting sore.

Between the workout and the damp, cool ocean air rolling in off the harbour, I was suddenly famished. My stomach growled like there was a wolverine down there.

In the mess hall, a row of cooks standing at a long cafeteria-style counter were serving up mountains of food.

I almost started to drool. "Wow, that's more food than I've seen in one place since last Christmas!"

"That's more food than I've *ever* seen, period!" said a guy from Ottawa named Finn, who wore a threadbare wool jacket and patched-up trousers.

"Bacon, sausage, eggs, toast, oatmeal, beans, juice!" he continued. "This is one line I don't mind being in."

"Damn right," said Ken. "Let's dive in before it's all gone."

The food was good, and we were ready for it. We could have whatever we wanted, and as much as we wanted. The cooks would dish it out from behind the counter, whatever we asked for. There were rows and rows of tables and benches. We found a space, sat down and devoured our breakfasts like a pack of ravenous wolves. Nobody talked until we'd finished everything on our plates.

After breakfast the petty officers led us back out to the parade ground. This time it was for marching drill, learning how to move in formation. For the next few days our waking hours were a monotonous routine of marching, calisthenics, parade-ground drill and then more marching, more calisthenics and more parade-ground drill, broken up only by sleep and the welcome reprieve of breakfast, lunch and dinner. Many of us had grown up in a world where you couldn't always count on getting "three squares," so the certainty of regular meals was a comfort, even if we had to spend the rest of our time running and marching and sleeping in a hammock in an unheated hockey rink.

At the end of the week we finally got our uniforms, two per person. The uniform consisted of dark blue bell-bottomed trousers and a matching tunic with white trim that we wore over a white undershirt, topped off with a blue cap. We were all in a hurry to get into our new outfits and see what they looked like. Guys eagerly peeled off their civilian clothes — some of which were pretty beaten up — and put on the brand-new uniforms. The joke was that the Navy issued its uniforms in two sizes: too big and too small. But I didn't hear any complaints. "We look like real sailors now, don't we, O'Connell!" said Ken as he smoothed down the short tunic over his trousers.

I looked down at myself in the new uniform and couldn't help smiling. We all looked good.

A lot of the guys began experimenting with the caps, tilting them at different angles, trying to figure out which position made them look toughest or sharpest.

In the midst of this Petty Officer Lancaster entered. "All right, gentlemen, quit admiring yourselves and fall in." He shouted it like a command, but I could see that he had a very faint grin. I think he was pleased to see us looking like real sailors at last.

We lined up for inspection. One by one, Lancaster checked us over, commenting wryly when somebody had worn their cap at too rakish an angle, saying, "Sailor, why is your cap on that angle? You make me dizzy just looking at you," or "How come your cap is on the side of your head? You got a hole there you're trying to cover up? Straighten that out!"

Once Lancaster had thoroughly educated us on the ins and outs of how not to wear our uniforms, we were back to our usual routine of workouts and drills. Each day our run got a little bit longer. At first, the Navy-issue boots tortured all of us. The hard leather chafed and gave us blisters that we would pop each night with a needle.

But after a couple of weeks, either the leather softened or my skin got tougher, because I stopped getting blisters. I was getting used to running long distances every day, and I enjoyed being out and seeing the activity in the harbour.

It was constantly busy, day and night, like an anthill. Ships were always being loaded, no matter what time it was. Every available space was put to use. Unlike the lake freighters I worked on, when the holds of these ships were filled, the crews would start lashing cargo down to the deck. You name it — lumber, drums of gasoline, trucks, Jeeps. As I ran along the street with the other guys in my group, I even saw a crane lifting the wingless fuselage of a large combat plane — everything from the nose and cockpit all the way back to the tail — toward a freighter. It was part of a Lockheed Hudson, one of the new twin-engine bombers built in the United States. It was so big it had to be disassembled to fit onto the cargo ship. I watched, feeling every twitch as the crane operator skilfully manoeuvred the large but fragile load toward the freighter. I breathed a sigh of relief when it touched down gently on the deck. The dock workers quickly began covering the plane with tarpaulins to protect it against the salt spray, then lashed it down. The instant they were finished, the crane operator began lowering an armoured personnel carrier toward them.

The length of the run was increased every day, so no matter how fit we got, by the end of the circuit there would always be a few guys throwing up on the pavement or into the bushes. Toward the end of our longest run, 8 miles, one of the fellows was suddenly overcome and almost vomited onto the feet of an expensively dressed woman out walking a miniature terrier. She curled up her lip and pulled her little dog closer. Then she screwed up her face and made a noise that sounded like "harumph."

Only a week before, the Halifax-based destroyer *Saguenay* had been torpedoed off Ireland while escorting a convoy. The *Saguenay* made it to port, but with a loss of twenty-one dead crew members. It was very much on our minds, but certainly didn't seem to be on hers.

From somewhere in our ranks a voice called out, "Don't worry, lady! If the Führer tries to move into your house, we'll do a lot more than just puke on him." The woman turned and strutted away, the sour expression still on her face.

"No need to thank us!" shouted Finn.

For some reason, the citizens of Halifax didn't seem too thrilled to see us. They would usually avoid our gaze when we passed them on the street. Nobody waved or cheered us on. I couldn't understand why they behaved that way. We were there to fight for their freedom, but they acted like we were invisible . . . or at least they wished we were.

* * *

When our six weeks of basic training were over, we began to specialize. Because I already had experience on lake freighters as a cook, that's where they wanted to put me, on a destroyer and out to sea right away. I protested. I was eager to do my part, but I hadn't quit my job as a cook on a freighter and come all this way just to cook meals and scrub pots for a bunch of other guys who were going to get all the action and glory.

I explained to Petty Officer Lancaster that I had done a lot of hunting and was good with a rifle. I told him that I had done well on the geometry and spatial relations portion of my intelligence tests too.

He took it all in with a pained expression, then replied, "Listen, Deadeye, if you really think you're that dangerous, you can join the other guys who are starting small-arms specialist training tomorrow. We'll see what you can do."

Early the next morning Lancaster led me out

onto the rifle range. It was cold and damp. Fog was rolling in from the ocean. Not the greatest conditions. But then, in combat, conditions would rarely be ideal either. Lancaster held a Lee Enfield .303 infantry rifle, similar to the old bolt-action rifle that my father and brothers and I shared back in Iroquois, except this one held a military ammunition clip that contained ten rounds, so I wouldn't have to stop and reload after each shot.

"Okay, let's see what you can do with this," he said, handing the gun to me.

I felt the weight of the Lee Enfield, noted the slightly different balance it had compared to my family's rifle. I checked it over, and when I felt familiar enough with it, I lay down on the field. The ground was damp and cold, and I took several deep, slow breaths to relax my muscles and keep my body steady, despite the chilly air. I knew that shivering would throw my aim off.

I raised the rifle at the target, which was a set of concentric circles printed on paper, propped up against an earthen wall 200 yards across the field. I took a moment to clear my thoughts and slow down my breathing, the way I did when I was hunting. I took aim at the target, then exhaled, and at the end of my breath, when my chest was motionless, squeezed the trigger. An instant later a loud *crack* of gunfire sounded and the butt of the rifle kicked back into my shoulder.

Lancaster peered at the target through his binoculars, then handed them to me. I took a look. I'd hit the target, but on the outer ring. Better than a newbie for sure, but outside the kill zone and not exactly impressive. The bullet had gone low and to the right of where I'd actually aimed. I handed the binoculars back to Lancaster. If I didn't do better, I'd end up in the galley for the rest of the war. But I pushed that kind of thought away so I could focus.

Part of being a good marksman is knowing how to correct for the inaccuracies of your rifle. I knew I had aimed slightly above the target to compensate for the bullet drop — the effect of gravity pulling the bullet down. But the other quirks of the gun had thrown off the shot. To compensate, this time I would aim higher and very slightly to the left of my target. It was a gamble, because I knew I wouldn't get another chance. I aimed, let out my breath and squeezed the trigger. There was another metallic *crack*. Without stopping, I chambered another bullet. I sighted exactly the same as before, let out my breath, then gently squeezed the trigger. I repeated the sequence until I had fired three more bullets.

Lancaster looked carefully at the target through

the binoculars, then handed them to me. "Have a look," he said.

I had shot two bulls' eyes and put the other rounds less than 4 inches from the centre of the target, well inside the kill zone.

"You gonna admire those holes all day, or can I have my binoculars back now?" said Lancaster.

"Yes, sir," I replied, handing them up to him.

"All right, O'Connell, you can get up off the ground. Looks like you might be useful for something other than peeling potatoes after all. I'm recommending you for gunnery school."

"Thank you, sir," I said, clambering to my feet. I tried not to show my excitement, but I was so thrilled I felt like I'd jump right out of my skin.

So instead of being immediately posted to a ship to start cooking, I began a gunnery course in Halifax. Ken made it in too, on the basis of his geometry aptitude and having been on his school's archery team.

Over the next few months we learned how to use every gun in the Navy's arsenal. The smallest was the Lewis gun, which was intended for anti-aircraft defence and close combat against the crews of surfaced submarines. It was a light machine gun left over from the First World War, firing the same ammunition that another Canadian, Roy Brown, had used to shoot down the Red Baron more than twenty years earlier. It might have been adequate to bring down a tiny, old-fashioned plane like the Baron's, made from wood and fabric. But it was a museum piece by Second World War standards. It used the same calibre bullets that my brothers and I shot deer and moose with, and had a maximum range of only a couple thousand feet and change. If you were close enough, you might kill the crew of a surfaced U-boat or prevent them from getting to their own guns. But against a heavily armoured German bomber, it was just about useless. For all practical purposes, they might as well have issued us a big sack of rocks to throw.

We also learned how to use the 4-inch and the 4.7-inch guns, the Royal Canadian Navy's main weapons on the corvettes and destroyers. We could never go into combat against a battleship or a cruiser with them — they'd be using their 11-inch guns — but they packed enough punch to send a German submarine straight to Davy Jones' locker, and that's exactly what corvettes were designed to do.

That didn't mean the submarines were a push-over, though, even on the surface. The U-boats were equipped with an 88-millimetre deck gun that was only slightly smaller in diameter than ours and could easily sink a merchantman —

or a corvette whose crew wasn't accurate or fast enough with its own deck gun.

On that last point, we were at a disadvantage. Like so much of our other equipment, our guns were proof of our government's stubborn refusal to prepare for war. The breech-loading 4-inch gun was an outdated relic from the First World War. Its shells weren't all one solid piece as in more modern guns. There was a projectile *and* a separate bag filled with an explosive called cordite, plus a cartridge like a shotgun shell filled with gunpowder to ignite the cordite, which in turn fired the warhead. The U-boats' 88-millimetre guns used shells that came with the firing charge built into them at the factory, like a bullet, so they didn't need to stuff a bag of cordite into their guns to propel the warhead, or insert a gunpowder firing cartridge to ignite the cordite. A surfaced U-boat could fire a 20-pound shell every four seconds or so — fifteen a minute — a lot faster than we could with our cumbersome old guns. But our instructors were first-rate. They drilled us constantly, so we had lots of practice. We might not have been able to fire our shells as quickly as a U-boat crew could, but we were determined that each one of ours would count.

Finally, after months of practice on the various guns, we were deemed ready for combat service.

Chapter Three
Spring 1941

With my gunnery training complete, my first official duty was to become part of the crew on the maiden voyage of the *Wildrose*, a corvette that had just been built at the shipyard in Sorel, on the St. Lawrence River between Montreal and Trois-Rivières. A few of the guys from my gunnery class made the trip with me, including Ken.

When our train arrived in Sorel, we boarded a military transport that carried us straight to the docks. I scrambled down from the truck, eager to see the ship on which I would make my first Atlantic crossing. But when I laid eyes on the *Wildrose* the only thing I felt was disappointment. We all did. A lot of the guys just threw down their kit bags and stared.

"Rub a dub-dub," I said.

"No kidding," replied Ken. "Good thing the Krauts are under water in their submarines. If they saw this thing, they'd be laughing at us."

Compared to other combat vessels, the *Wildrose* didn't look like a thoroughbred at all. She was clearly built neither for speed nor beauty, with a squat, rounded hull and a stern that looked a bit like a bathtub. For an ocean-going ship, she wasn't very long, either. Even in the sheltered waters of the dockyard, with just a slight breeze and light waves, the *Wildrose* rolled slightly from side to side.

"She's based on a whaling ship design," said one of the other sailors, a guy from Quebec City named Fontaine. "They can build them quicker and cheaper than any of the other types of ships."

I tried to keep an open mind, but standing there taking in the sight of the *Wildrose*, those seemed like its only positive attributes.

The worst moment came when I glanced at the forward deck. "Hey, Ken, notice anything unusual about her?" I asked.

"Other than the fact that she looks like a giant chum bucket that could capsize on wet grass?"

"Guess again," I said.

"Holy smoke!" he exclaimed as he followed my gaze to a crane that was hoisting a grey telephone pole to the mounting, right where the 4-inch gun — the only sizeable weapon on the ship — was supposed to be.

"You don't think they're serious, do you, O'Connell?" he asked. Shipyard workers lowered the telephone pole toward the *Wildrose*'s deck and guided it into the steel gun mount.

"Doesn't look to me like they're kidding," I replied.

Then the workers bolted the pole into place so it looked like a gun barrel. "What the heck is with the pole?" I asked one of them.

"No more guns," he replied in a French-Canadian accent. "Nobody makes them here in Canada. On the first corvettes we built, we got old artillery pieces taken from the the lawns of the Legion Halls. Then we even ran out of those. There's not a gun left on any Legion Hall in the country. Guess you guys should have joined up sooner."

"Lord love a duck," said Ken, shaking his head.

So for its maiden voyage, the only working guns on the entire vessel were the two small-calibre Lewis machine guns. Being a cook on a destroyer was suddenly looking pretty good compared to being on this poor excuse for a ship. If a U-boat came to the surface beyond the range of our Lewis guns, we'd have no way to protect ourselves except for a telephone pole disguised to look like a gun to hide our near-defencelessness.

As we stepped onto the gangplank it occurred to me that this series of ship was called a "Flower-class" corvette. Mistake number one, I thought.

Other ships were named after fierce tribes, like the Zulu and Ashanti, or warrior traits like Courageous or Indomitable, even tenacious or ferocious animals like Bulldog or Basilisk. But our little bathtub of a ship, with nothing but two First World War-era machine guns to defend itself, was named after a *flower.* And not just any flower. A flower that grew on the *prairies*, thousands of miles from the nearest salt water. It all felt like a giant joke. A joke that wasn't funny.

I stepped off the gangplank onto the deck. The ship was a hive of activity. Most of the crew were already at their stations, preparing the ship for sea. There was no speech from the captain or anything like that. The chief petty officer told us where to stow our kit. We ducked through a hatch and went down a flight of metal stairs into the forward mess deck, a dimly lit area near the bow of the ship, just underneath what would have been the forward gun station — if we'd *had* a gun. There were tables and benches around the outside with lids that lifted to double as storage lockers. I found a spot to hang up my hammock, then stowed my other gear in one of the benches.

By the time our crew took over the *Wildrose*, the shipyard workers had already tested every part of the ship except for the weapons, so we were ready to take her out almost immediately. Once we were in the St. Lawrence, away from shore, we were told our destination: the port of Greenock, Scotland. There, *Wildrose* would get her 4-inch gun. The captain ordered the engine to be gradually powered up to maximum speed. Those of us who had never before served on a corvette, which was most of the crew, were puzzled. We were going pretty slowly.

"You think there's something wrong with the engines, O'Connell?" Ken asked.

A passing stoker overheard us and shook his head. "Nothing wrong with the engines. This is all she's got. A corvette will only do sixteen knots under full steam."

That's about 18 miles an hour — the same speed as somebody riding a bicycle, or half the speed of a destroyer, not much faster than a submerged U-boat, and actually slightly *slower* than a surfaced German submarine.

Ken and I rolled our eyes. He leaned over to me and whispered, "Jeez, O'Connell, is this what we're supposed to take on the Krauts with? A chum bucket with a telephone pole?"

He didn't say it in his usual smart-alecky way.

"Looks that way to me," I replied.

He shook his head. "Then God help us all."

It would be at least a day until we were past Quebec City and could safely test fire the Lewis guns. Given that, plus the fact that the ship was brand new and not in need of maintenance, there was very little for me to do. The Navy brass considered corvettes too small to have a trained cook on them, and after the second time that we were served peanut butter on toast in the same day, I realized the guys in the kitchen needed some help. So even though I had specifically taken on gun training to avoid "kitchen patrol," I found myself back in the galley.

The kitchen was about the same size as the cooking area in typical family home. It had a four-burner stove, an oven and a countertop about 6 feet long, which was the only workspace. There was no refrigerator, so a lot of the food was canned, like tomatoes, green beans and corn, plus fresh root vegetables that wouldn't spoil quickly, like potatoes, carrots and onions. There was also lots of jam and margarine, and something called ship's biscuit, a cracker that was dry and hard so it didn't go bad in the moist air.

The corvette was originally designed to carry a crew of about seventy, but with all the wartime gear, and operating on a twenty-four-hour-a-day basis for an Atlantic crossing, it needed close to one hundred men to keep it running. That meant it was already overcrowded with the crew and all their gear, plus the food needed to feed so many people for the two-week crossing. So the provisions were crammed into every nook and cranny, even stored in the sick bay, just down the hall from the galley.

As part of the gun crew, I shared lookout duty. Once a day I spent an hour in the crow's nest about 30 feet above the deck. I got my first taste of that job the morning after we left Sorel. The petty officer woke me just before dawn. One of the things about Navy life that most people found hardest to adjust to, including me, were the four-hour watches — being on duty for four hours, then off duty for four hours. From the captain on down to the lowliest ordinary seaman, nobody ever got more than four hours of uninterrupted sleep. It always seemed that just when I was finally asleep and oblivious to the clanging, the voices, the rumble of the engines, a petty officer would give me a nudge and tell me it was time to get up.

When I opened my eyes the mess deck was dim, lit only by blue lights that were kept low to make it tolerable for people who were trying to sleep. I climbed out of my hammock, in full uniform. We learned right away that everyone always slept with their clothes on, because we never knew when there might be an emergency. The last thing we wanted to do, especially in the icy North Atlantic, was to go into combat in our underwear!

I made my way to the galley, where the fellow who was on duty as cook handed me a steaming cup of tea. He didn't have any cooking experience, so my breakfast was a ship's biscuit with jam. We were still in the St. Lawrence and the water this morning was calm. The sky was just beginning to get light, with a faint rim of red above the eastern horizon. The countryside was beginning to emerge from the dark. Here and there, I could make out the silhouettes of farmhouses and barns on either side of the river, and little villages that reminded me of Iroquois.

About half an hour into my watch, the cliffs of Quebec City came into view, glinting golden as they caught the first rays of morning sun. Toward the end of my stint atop the crow's nest we passed beneath the Plains of Abraham. The ancient battlefield where General Wolfe's army had defeated Montcalm's now looked so deserted and peaceful, it was hard to believe that a battle that decided the fate of North America had taken place there. It occurred to me for the first time that lots of the guys I was fighting alongside were descendants of people who had fought on both sides of that conflict. And now here we were, depending on each other for survival, fighting together against an enemy far more ruthless than anyone our ancestors had faced.

Soon the river began to widen, giving a breathtaking view out toward the Gulf of St. Lawrence. I was actually a little disappointed when it was time to come down and let the next guy take over the watch duties.

An hour or so later we passed Grosse-Île. It gave me a melancholy feeling. My O'Connell grandparents and great-grandparents had come to Canada together as refugees from Ireland during the Potato Famine a century earlier, crammed into what were called coffin ships. According to stories I'd heard passed down through my family, so many people died on their ship and were buried at sea that sharks began to follow it. My great-grandmother was terrified of dying at sea and being eaten by those sharks. She almost made it to Canada, but caught typhus within sight of land, died within days and was buried right over there on Grosse-Île. It gave me a wistful feeling to know that somewhere on that lonely looking island she lay buried far from her loved ones in an unmarked grave.

And I thought about those sharks. But not for long, because the shoreline was growing distant, so we could now safely test fire our guns. Ken and I practised by shooting at the whitecaps on the waves. Just like that day out on the rifle range, I had to get a feel for the quirks of this gun. With a few minutes' practice I was able to hit my targets accurately. I now felt ready to take on the Kriegsmarine and the Luftwaffe — at least if we could ever get close enough.

Late that day when we reached the mouth of the Saguenay River, the man in the crow's nest shouted, "Whales!" A pod of belugas skimmed the surface as they came up to chase small fish. The largest was as big as a car and looked like a giant, white ghost as it glided effortlessly just beneath the waves. They swam right beside us on a parallel course for about five minutes, before veering off and diving away. As I stood by the railing watching them fade from sight, the spray from a wave splashed onto my face. I ran my tongue across my lips and tasted salt in the water. The St. Lawrence, the familiar river that I'd spent my entire life on, was giving way to the ocean.

Next morning when I woke in the gloom of the mess deck, I knew immediately that something had changed. The ceiling, just above my head, was tilting on much steeper angles than when I'd climbed into my hammock. The *Wildrose* pitched up and down along its length, climbing over each wave, then dropping down the other side before starting the whole process all over again. There was a yaw too as the bow swung slightly from left to right. I felt a slight queasiness in my own stomach just as I caught a whiff of vomit. With the waves growing larger and choppier, people were beginning to get seasick.

The hatches had been closed because of the rougher seas and the air was heavy with the breath of fifty men sleeping in an enclosed space. Fumes from the paint and solvents that were stored beneath us in the bowels of the ship were blending in with the smell of the puke and the stale air. The queasy feeling in my stomach got more intense. It wasn't quite time for my watch to start, but I had to get some fresh air. I slid out of my hammock and put my feet down. As soon as I felt the ship rocking and bobbing beneath me, the urge to throw up became uncontrollable.

I raced down the narrow corridor and up toward the main deck. I made it outside just in time to vomit over the railing and down the side of the ship. I hung there, puking, till I thought my guts would fall out. When there was nothing left to come up I grabbed my kit, went into one of the tiny, cramped washroom stalls and brushed

my teeth, trying to get the taste of bile out. I even put some toothpaste on my finger and rubbed it around in my mouth, but the taste was still there, and I was so queasy that even having my finger touch my tongue made me gag.

Because my stomach was still churning, I took my turn in the crow's nest without eating breakfast. It was swaying from side to side at the top of the mast like an amusement park ride. I felt the nausea building again. Down below, a couple of other guys next to the depth-charge racks were throwing up over the stern. Just then my stomach started heaving. I looked over the rail again but the bridge was immediately below me. I figured that barfing onto the captain or the first mate would be frowned upon, so as the scorching vomit surged up my throat, I pulled off my cap and threw up into it. It was disgusting, but there was no other choice.

For the rest of my watch I had to hang on to the crow's nest railing with one hand and my cap with the other so the puke that filled it wouldn't spill onto the officers on the deck below. After that my stomach settled down a bit and I could concentrate on my job.

We were now so far out in the Gulf that no land was in sight. For all I knew, there could be a submarine out there right now, waiting for a chance to slam a torpedo into us. So despite the constant pitching, I managed to suppress the nausea and ride out the rest of my shift.

We joined up with an eastbound convoy in St. John's, Newfoundland. All forty merchant ships in it were heavily loaded. Some had lumber lashed to the decks; others carried trucks and airplanes — I could make out their shapes under the tarpaulins. On one big freighter, a row of tanks was lashed down, gun barrels poking out from under their coverings.

Ken couldn't resist another remark. "Jeez, O'Connell," he said, "too bad we couldn't carry one of those tanks. Then we'd have a gun to shoot!"

Oil tankers were positioned here and there throughout the convoy and, in the middle of an inner row, was another tanker that we had been told carried high-octane aviation fuel for Spitfire fighter planes. Ken wasn't so smart-alecky now.

"I hope we don't have to get too close to that one," he said. "If it takes a torpedo, it'll go up like a bomb!"

"Just imagine the poor bastards who have to sail her, and be glad you're not one of them," commented a voice behind us.

I turned and saw that it was our captain.

"Yes, sir!" we both said, saluting.

The captain made no further comment and continued on his way. Suddenly I was especially glad I'd made a point of vomiting into my cap instead of onto the bridge.

Heading east, we were soon south of Greenland. The waves were relentless, but after a few days at sea everyone in the crew gradually became used to the motion and our seasickness subsided. I conducted regular maintenance of the Lewis guns, making sure the salt water was cleaned off them, and shooting into the wavetops for practice.

Much more impressive were the depth-charge drills. The charges were our main anti-submarine weapon. Each one, looking like an oil drum, was packed with 300 pounds of explosives. Its fuse was controlled by the amount of water pressure, so it could be set to detonate at a particular depth, usually 50 feet. They were rolled off a rail at the back of the ship, above where we hoped the submarine would be if our ASDIC operators had been able to track the sub accurately.

On this occasion, the crew was given a hypothetical depth and bearing. The explosion when the first pattern of depth charges detonated behind us was spectacular. The ocean boiled up and out of it shot a huge column of white water 60 feet into the air. The shock wave rattled the hull, and even the steel deck beneath my feet. After that I was feeling a little more confident about our chances against a U-boat, as long as we caught it underwater and kept it there.

When we reached the mid-Atlantic we had a couple of days of heavy rains. That's when I discovered one of the least likeable features of the corvette. To get our food, we had to walk through an open area between the galley and the mess deck. This wasn't such a problem in fine weather. But if it was raining, or the sea was choppy, the food would get covered in water, and it was hard even keeping it on your plate.

One stormy afternoon when we were getting our lunch, Fontaine was right in front of me, carrying a plate of canned sausages, when he slipped and fell and the sausages went flying.

"*Tabouère!*" he cursed. Then he picked them up, looked at them and went to wipe them off on his oilskin.

"Careful," I said, "I've done that. That just makes them even dirtier."

We laughed. He held the sausages out over the railing, where the salt spray washed at least some of the gunk off them.

"Better cold than covered in diesel oil," he said. He popped one in his mouth and we kept on going.

I also quickly learned why our corvette was known as a "wet" ship, and it wasn't just because of the effect on the food. Even with the hatches closed, there was always water leaking in from somewhere below deck. It dripped down onto us while we slept in our hammocks. After a storm, so much water sloshed around the mess deck that it would soak everything in our lockers. I had to master the art of sleeping in wet clothes, under a wet blanket. Fortunately, because they were wool, they would warm up quickly, so I tried to think of it as a hot, wet cocoon. There was no room for washing facilities like on bigger ships. We did our best using buckets and rags, but before long, we were filthy. The stink in the mess deck became so bad, I got used to breathing through my mouth, just so I wouldn't have to smell it.

Early one morning, after nearly two weeks of working, eating and sleeping in wet clothing, we heard a shout from the crow's nest. "Ireland! I can see the coast!"

A cheer went up throughout the ship.

We were all ecstatic, but so exhausted and sleep deprived that seeing that emerald strip of land rising out of the steely grey water felt like a dream.

A career petty officer warned us, "All right, lads! We're almost there. But don't let your guard down. Even this close to port, there can be U-boats on the prowl. And now we're in range of the Jerry bombers, so keep your eyes peeled."

"What do you say, O'Connell," Ken quipped. "Shall we go upstairs and check the peashooters?"

"Good idea," I replied. Then we climbed up to the gun positions and test fired a few rounds on the Lewis machine guns. But despite the threat of German bombers, I knew we would soon be ashore, and I had to conceal my excitement.

The next day we steamed up the Firth of Clyde to the base at Greenock, one of the main assembly points for the North Atlantic convoys. It was filled with British battleships, cruisers and everything on down, all of them bristling with guns. One of them was absolutely massive.

A sub-lieutenant noticed me watching and filled us in. "That's the *Prince of Wales*," he said. "Seven hundred and forty-five feet long. She'll do twenty-eight knots under full steam." Twenty-eight knots — more than thirty miles an hour — was an impressive speed for a craft the length of three city blocks. The *Prince of Wales* weighed forty times more than the *Wildrose*, yet was nearly twice as fast. Its ten 14-inch guns looked incredibly powerful. Next to it, our corvette seemed like an overgrown bathtub toy, especially when the Royal Navy sailors lined up for inspection on the battleship's deck in their crisp blue uniforms, while we wore our sweaty, filthy, slept-in clothing. I felt like a naïve, pathetic colonial who was lucky to have made it across the Atlantic alive.

Chapter Four
Mid-April 1941

Greenock was where we and HMCS *Wildrose* were to part company. The ship would now be sent into the dockyard, where workers would fit it up with its 4-inch gun. There was no time for us to wait around. There were convoys returning to North America, and other escort ships in need of fresh crews. So we assumed that we'd be reassigned to a different ship, hopefully to something more potent this time, like a destroyer.

Meanwhile the base at Greenock was well equipped, and we were at last able to wash up and get into some clean clothes. After we did, we stowed our kit and explored the town.

"This is amazing," I said to Ken. "I've heard more languages spoken in the first ten minutes here than I've heard in my entire life."

The place was buzzing with sailors whose countries had been overrun by the Nazis, but who had chosen to leave their families and homelands behind to come here and fight on. There were French, Dutch, Poles, Norwegians, Danes and

Greeks in addition to us Canadians, the New Zealanders, the Aussies and the Brits.

Interesting as Greenock was, Glasgow, the biggest city in Scotland, was just up the river and that was too tempting to resist. Ken and I boarded a train in Greenock and in less than an hour had reached downtown Glasgow. The streets were bustling and full of life. People were shopping, working, going about their business. I immediately noticed that sailors and other armed forces personnel mixed with the civilians. It wasn't like Halifax, where the local people avoided us, and we sailors were expected to keep to our own area. Even so, I was surprised when a woman carrying groceries paused, took a look at our shoulder flashes and said, "Good to have you here, Canada." Then she reached out and touched both our collars in turn.

"Thanks, glad to be here," I said. I was happy for the warm welcome, but a bit taken aback. Still, it was a nice change from Halifax.

"Funny the way she touched our collars," said Ken.

"Yes," I replied. "Maybe we remind her of her sons?"

Ken grinned. "Then I must remind her of the handsome one."

"More likely the mouthy one," I replied.

We were eager to find something fun to do. The Navy hadn't provided any recreational facilities for us in Halifax. It had only one movie theatre so there were always long lineups. If we didn't get to the theatre well ahead of time, we usually couldn't get in. So Ken and I were glad to finally be in a place that was full of music, cafés and cinemas. Walking along a downtown street, we spotted a movie marquee and posters for not one but *two* movies that were playing simultaneously in separate theatres. The first was for a movie called *The Sea Wolf*. It was about people in dire circumstances on a sealing ship.

"Dire circumstances on a ship?" Ken snorted. "No thanks!"

"No kidding," I agreed. "We can get that for free on the *Wildrose*. We don't need to pay to see a movie about it."

Our eyes immediately drifted over to the other poster, for a movie called *High Sierra*. On it was a picture of an upcoming actor named Humphrey Bogart. He glared out from the poster with a tough-guy expression and held two Colt .45 calibre pistols, one in each hand.

"Jeez, that guy's packing more firepower than the entire *Wildrose*," I said.

"Maybe they should stick him in a canoe and send him out against the Krauts," Ken shot back.

We had a good laugh over that, then bought our tickets and got into line.

While we were standing there, an elderly man emerged from the busy pub next door. As he passed us he smiled and said, "Enjoy the film, Canada." He reached out and touched my collar, then ambled off down the street.

I looked at Ken. "That's really weird. That's the second time somebody's touched my collar since we got here."

Suddenly I heard a young woman's voice right behind me. "Didn't you know, Canada? It's good luck to touch a sailor's collar."

I turned and saw a girl about my age, grinning at me. I tripped over my words, but I managed to blurt out, "It's good luck?"

"Well, normally it is, but I suppose it depends on the sailor," she answered. She and her friend started to laugh. "So I hope you're lucky," she continued as she reached out and touched my collar.

"I hope so too," I said. "This is my shipmate, Ken Luke, and my name's Bill O'Connell."

"I'm Aileen Henderson, and this is Heather Murray," she responded.

"So what do you do on your ship?" Heather asked Ken.

"I'm a small-arms expert. Bill is our chief gunner."

"A gunner?" Aileen exclaimed. "Firing a big cannon? That's impressive," she said with a hint of mock admiration. "What kind is it?"

I started to answer, about to tell her that it would normally be a 4-inch gun.

But Ken jumped in. "Actually, Bill hasn't been given a gun yet."

I made a face at him to shut up, but Ken, being Ken, just kept going.

"We don't have any guns in Canada, so they installed a telephone pole in our turret to make it look like we're not defenceless. And they put Bill here in charge of it."

The girls grinned at each other. Aileen looked at me and raised an eyebrow. "Well, that must be quite a responsibility, keeping your telephone pole safe from Herr Hitler's navy."

I felt my face turning red. "Yeah . . . it, um, keeps me busy," I managed to say.

Just when I was beginning to feel like a fool, she rescued me. "Oh well, if you managed to make it all the way over here from Canada with nothing to defend yourself except a telephone pole, then you must have some luck for sure."

I liked Aileen already. She seemed different than the girls back in Iroquois, confident and outgoing. There was something mischievous and lively about her, and it made me want to get to know her better.

The line began to move and the four of us entered the theatre and sat down together on the soft, padded seats. After spending two weeks on the hard benches and my cold, wet hammock in the *Wildrose*, it was like being in a palace.

When the movie was over and the lights came back on, we stood up together and headed out through the lobby. When we stepped onto the street I was surprised at how dark it was. There were still people moving through the streets, but they were like ghostly shadows. I stopped in my tracks. I could hardly see a thing, let alone where I was stepping, because all the streetlights were off, and every curtain in every window was drawn closed.

"Wow," I said, "I've heard about blackouts in the newsreels, but I didn't realize they were this . . . " I searched for the word.

"Black?" joked Aileen. "We try not to make it too easy for the Luftwaffe to find us."

"How do you find *your* way around?" I asked.

"Oh, you get used to it. They tell us that if we eat enough carrots, we'll be able to see in the dark just like a cat."

"I didn't realize Scottish cats ate carrots," I replied. "At least I haven't seen any doing it so far."

"Well, stick around, Billy O'Connell. If the rationing gets any worse, you just might. First it was bacon, butter and sugar," she said. "But now it's almost everything. Meat, eggs, milk, biscuits. You can't get bananas or lemons at all anymore, and oranges hardly ever, even when you're sick."

But neither she nor I wanted to spend the night talking about not having enough to eat, or how bad things were. There was plenty of misery to go around on the *Wildrose*, and here in Glasgow I just wanted to have some fun.

We found a café, and except for the blackout curtains in the windows, I thought how similar it was to our diner back home in Iroquois. It even had the same model of Wurlitzer jukebox, and a Coca-Cola sign on the wall.

But it wasn't long after we sat down that I discovered there were some big differences too. When the waiter came over to take our order, I asked for a cheeseburger.

"Sorry, son, we haven't any meat," he replied. "Not with the rationing as it is."

Aileen recommended the fish and chips instead. It was delicious. The fish was so fresh, it reminded me of home. Afterward we had rhubarb pie, which in spite of the rationing was one treat they were still able to enjoy, since the rhubarb was grown there.

After dinner Ken and I walked Aileen and Heather home through the darkened streets. Finally we arrived at a corner where the girls said they had to split up. They lived only about three blocks from each other, so Ken and I agreed to meet back at the intersection in ten minutes. Then Aileen and I continued to her place. We walked down a long, narrow street that had two-storey brick row houses running down each side of it. After another block she stopped in front of one of them.

"Well, here we are, Billy O'Connell. Thank you for a pleasant evening."

"No, thank you," I said. "You have no idea how nice a change this was from the last two weeks."

"Well, I'm glad to hear that it was more enjoyable than sloshing around out there in the ocean with nothing but Ken and a telephone pole for company."

I laughed. "That's for sure!" Then I said, "Can I call you if I'm back this way?"

She hesitated a moment. "No, you can't. Sorry," she said, looking serious. I felt suddenly awkward. Was she telling me she didn't want to see me again? Then I saw a hint of a crooked grin. "Because we don't have a telephone. We're not like you wealthy Canadians, driving around in your Cadillacs and ringing people up willy-nilly."

I laughed again.

She turned and pointed to her house number. "Thirty-seven Bell Lane, speaking of phones. Just like Alexander Graham Bell, the fellow who invented them."

"That will be easy to remember," I replied. "Bell is one of the most famous *Canadians* ever."

"He wasn't a Canadian, I'll have you know. He was a *Scot*," said Aileen.

"Can't he be both?" I asked.

She raised an eyebrow. "I'll have to think on that one. Ask me next time I see you. When you're ready to get in touch, there's our ultra-modern communication device." She pointed toward the door knocker. "Now I've got to get my beauty rest so I can look good down at the ammunition factory."

I started to lean in to kiss her when she pulled back slightly and held out her hand.

"Good night, you wild Canadian."

Recovering, I reached out and took her hand. She squeezed mine gently. It was more than a handshake. She began to stroke my fingers. I pulled her close to me. I felt her warm breath on my neck. We stood like that in the doorway for a long moment. Then her gentle grasp lightened as she began to let go, and I knew it was time to say goodbye. She opened the front door and stepped into the darkened hallway.

"Safe travels!" she whispered.

"Take care," I said.

I smiled and waved as she closed the door. Then I carefully retraced my steps through the dark until I nearly bumped into Ken waiting on the corner.

"Did you kiss her?" he asked.

"None of your business," I replied.

"You didn't kiss her," he concluded, grinning.

"How do you know I didn't?" I asked.

"If you had," he replied, "you wouldn't say it was none of my business."

"Okay, so what about you, Mister Romance Expert?" I shot back. "Did you kiss Heather?"

"None of your business," he said.

We laughed, then walked off gingerly into the murky Glasgow night.

Eventually, after banging into numerous lamp-posts and newspaper boxes in the pitch black, we found a Salvation Army, which had clean, inexpensive beds and cheap meals for sailors, soldiers and airmen. We were given our bunks, and I enjoyed the luxury of not having to sleep fully clothed, tossed about in a wet hammock. I fell into a deep, deep sleep.

Chapter Five
Mid-April–mid-June 1941

When we returned to Greenock the next morning, I was expecting to join the rest of my crewmates from the *Wildrose* on a Royal Canadian Navy warship heading back to Halifax. But I discovered instead that I'd been assigned to take specialist gunnery training here on the base in Scotland. We knew the Royal Navy thought the standards of the RCN were inadequate, but evidently a British officer had seen the scores from the Halifax gunnery course and decided that Ken and I had potential. That meant for the next two months we would be based in Greenock, attending a training school. In truth, I was glad to get away from Halifax. In just two days ashore in Scotland, I'd had more pleasant interaction with civilians than in the entire time I'd spent in Halifax. And from what I'd seen, this base was far better equipped than we were, so it would be a chance to use top-notch gear instead of hand-me-downs from the last war. Besides that, staying behind in Scotland meant that I might have a chance to see Aileen again.

The gunnery school was far more sophisticated than anything the Canadian Navy possessed. We got to use a shore-based indoor gun deck designed to simulate shipboard conditions, to give each student the maximum amount of practice time. It was rigged hydraulically to pitch up and down, just like a real ship. That way we could practise compensating for the motion of the waves. It was uncanny how realistic the movement was. We drilled for hours and hours in that room, and with time, got quicker and more accurate, despite the unpredictability of the movement beneath our feet.

They kept us busy with live-firing exercises too, in the open ocean northwest of Scotland. Our instructors taught us things that we couldn't have learned ashore, like how to compensate not just for the rolling of the ship, but also for the wind and for atmospheric pressure, both of which can throw even a big shell off course by the time it has travelled a few miles. On our live-fire exercises a tugboat would approach, towing a wooden target. When it got within range, we would be given the order to fire. With the constant drilling and instruction from our Royal Navy teachers, we got to the point where we were consistently accurate. After a few weeks, even in rough waters, we usually only had to fire one shell to get the range of our target, then could hit it on most of the subsequent shots.

Finally one evening when the tug came into view, we judged the distance so correctly, compensated for the wind, waves and pressure so accurately that we hit the target on our first shot, blowing it into splinters. Our lieutenant, a Royal Navy man with a thick Liverpool accent, gazed at the remains of the target through his binoculars, then looked at us. "Not bad," he said. "We just might make something of you colonials yet. Carry on."

We were thrilled. Despite his aloofness, we knew we'd impressed the pants off him.

I was also tested for suitability as a specialist anti-aircraft gunner. I was led into a darkened room and handed a BB gun. Then small model airplanes appeared randomly out of the dark at the end of a mechanical arm. I had only an instant to identify each and decide if it was German or Allied and whether to fire at it or not. I'd lose points if I didn't hit the German planes, and I'd fail the test if I shot at our own planes.

I had memorized the aircraft identification charts in advance, but the decisions were split second and it was hard to prepare. A model of a German Heinkel 111 bomber swung across the ceiling out of the gloom. I led it with my gun the same way I used to lead ducks when Dad and I were out hunting. I squeezed the trigger. A red light blinked on to indicate a hit.

Next came a Lockheed Hudson bomber, a type that often flew escort cover for our ships partway into the Atlantic. I held my fire.

Then a big four-engine bomber zoomed across the ceiling. In the dim light it had a passing resemblance to our own Boeing Flying Fortress. I hesitated a moment, then caught the unmistakable silhouette of the gunner's gondola that hung beneath it. It was a Luftwaffe Focke-Wulf 200. I squeezed the trigger and managed to get two shots in.

Two more planes flew past, a Catalina patrol plane and a Sunderland flying boat. I held my fire. At last a twin-engine bomber swooped in out of the dark. Like the larger Focke-Wulf, it had a gondola for a gunner under the nose. A German Junkers Ju 88 bomber. I got a clean shot in on one of its two engines.

The instructor entered and announced that the test was over. He led me out of the room. When I emerged I discovered that quite few of the guys had washed out for shooting at the Allied planes.

Ken was waiting for his turn. He wanted to be an anti-aircraft gunner too, but I knew he hadn't studied the aircraft charts the way I had. He looked at me with a "Help!" expression. The instructor had taken the next candidate in, so I leaned over and whispered, "Heinkel, Hudson, Fw 200, Catalina, Sunderland, Ju 88." He nodded without answering.

Later that day we discovered we'd both passed the test.

Ken cheered, then slapped me on the shoulder and leaned in close.

"Thanks, O'Connell," he said. "I'd never have recognized those planes if you hadn't told me the order they were in."

I'd saved him before the test, but I wasn't going to let him off the hook now. "You're welcome," I replied. "But you've got to study those charts till you know them inside out. If you shoot down one of our guys by mistake, it's on *my* head now because I got you in."

"Don't worry," he said. "I promise I'll bone up on the identification charts. At least, if you pull your head out of them long enough to let the rest of us guys take a look."

A couple of days later we were sent to a Royal Navy air gunnery school, where we practised with the familiar old .303 Lewis gun. It was no better suited to anti-aircraft service than when I'd first begun training, but at least the British gave us a chance to try it out under more realistic conditions. At sea, a specially armoured airplane would tow a target at the end of a long steel cable. We would try to get as many strikes in on the target as we could before it was hauled away. Later our instructors would count the number of holes in the target and compare it to the amount of ammunition we'd fired to see how accurate we were.

I also was trained on the Oerlikon 20-millimetre cannon, a new weapon just coming into service. It was far superior to the Lewis gun. It fired automatically like a machine gun, but the shells were ten times heavier than the bullets in the Lewis, and exploded on impact. They gave us massive striking power compared to a machine gun and had twice the range. They could be used when planes were so close that the big guns couldn't track them accurately. With an Oerlikon, we could punch a hole right through a sub's conning tower. I liked the Oerlikon. Soon I was proficient with it and could blast a tug target to smithereens. It felt good to use a weapon with some real punch. I knew that after this there would no more telephone-pole guns for me.

That was a good thing, because out in the North Atlantic, things were really heating up. On Sunday, May 25, we learned that the *Bismarck*, one of the Nazis' newest and largest battleships, had been intercepted attempting to break out into the Atlantic to sink Allied merchant ships. In the confrontation it had sunk the British battlecruiser HMS *Hood* with what the Admiralty called a "lucky hit," taking more than 1400 sailors to their graves. The news of such a tremendous loss was shocking and a huge blow to Allied morale. The British were determined not to let this go unanswered, and were even more determined not to let the *Bismarck* get near the Allied shipping lanes. Two days later, a combination of British ships and aircraft sank the *Bismarck*, which went down with a loss of over 2000 German sailors.

I was itching to try out my newly honed gunnery skills on the enemy, but that hadn't happened yet. There may have been epic battles unfolding out in the Atlantic, and Liverpool and Belfast had been bombed heavily that month by the Luftwaffe, but for me, the skies and seas were maddeningly empty of Nazis. The German Navy and Air Force were beginning to seem almost imaginary, more like a bogeyman under the bed than a real danger.

On one training mission a twin-engine plane came over the horizon heading in our general direction.

"That's odd. The target tug isn't due here for

another eleven minutes," said a petty officer.

"There's a convoy heading west from Ireland now. Could be one of the escort bombers making a rendezvous," said a sub-lieutenant.

The plane made an abrupt change of course, darted into a cloud bank, and we lost visual contact with it. I thought it was suspicious behaviour for a friendly aircraft to suddenly change direction and hide itself like that, so I kept my eye on the clouds. Having noted the plane's speed, I tried to estimate where it might reappear. The officers didn't seem too concerned and went about their business. But I continued to mentally picture where it would be in the cloud bank. About forty-five seconds later I spotted the same plane emerging from the clouds, one nautical mile ahead, in a shallow dive toward us. It looked to be travelling at over 200 miles an hour, and at that speed, could close the distance in under twenty seconds. There was little time to think it over.

"It's a friendly. Looks like a Blenheim," I heard someone say.

Its angle of approach didn't seem very friendly to me. The nose-on orientation made it impossible to see any wing markings and tell if it was German or British.

I squinted to make out the glassed-in nose and

cockpit and the radial engines. The Blenheim had those features, but this plane also had a gondola under the nose for a gunner. I knew my identification charts. This was no Blenheim.

I released the safety on the Oerlikon and began to track it, aiming not at it, but slightly below and ahead, to match its rate of descent.

In my peripheral vision, I noticed the petty officer raising his binoculars to take a closer look. A moment later he shouted, "Damn, it's a Junkers 88!"

I didn't hesitate. I squeezed the trigger. A stream of red tracers erupted out of my gun toward the German bomber. The first few shells passed beneath the plane. By this time its nose gunner was firing at us with a machine gun. His bullets whizzed past me and made a metallic clatter like hail as they ricocheted off our funnel. He was trying to force us to take cover and keep us away from our own weapons so the plane could press home its attack and drop its bombs on us.

"Not today, you don't," I muttered. I wasn't going to let this gunner scatter me or the other crew. I fired a burst and saw yellow flashes as my shells slammed into the gunner's position and exploded. Bits of glass and metal flew off the plane. Its machine-gun fire abruptly stopped.

But the bomber kept on coming straight at me. I adjusted my aim, fired again. Now yellow flashes burst on the leading edges of the wings as several of my shells scored direct hits. A few more shots like that, and I'd blast this bird right out of the sky.

The pilot must have known too, because he immediately took evasive action, turning hard to starboard. As the plane banked I saw the Swastika on its tail and the black Iron Crosses on the underside of its wings.

The German pilot was good. He manoeuvred his plane so violently, skidding and yawing, I thought he would tear the wings right off it. It was almost impossible to track his course now, it had become so unpredictable. But I continued to lay down a curtain of fire and managed to score one more solid hit. A big chunk of sheet metal flew off his tail rudder where my parting shot had slammed into it. Good, I thought. He'll be so busy just trying to keep his plane in the air that he won't be able to attack any other Allied ships.

By now our other guns had opened up on him as well. The Lewis guns were spewing streams of bullets enthusiastically if ineffectively, and the 4-inch gun was loaded with an anti-aircraft shell and being swung into position. When one of those shells exploded not far from the Ju 88 several seconds later, it must have been all the discouragement the pilot needed. He released his bombs into the ocean to lighten the damaged plane and make it easier to control. Then he hightailed it for home, skimming the wavetops.

My pulse was racing. This had been my first real test. I hadn't crumpled under the pressure, and I had survived. I hadn't shot the plane down, but I'd prevented it from sinking us. I'd damaged it badly enough that it would tie up German repair crews and keep it from attacking anyone else for a few days. I wondered what had become of the German nose gunner, and realized how easily it could have been the other way around. But I realized something else too: if I hadn't trusted my instincts and taken the initiative to defend myself, there was a good chance that the plane would have dropped its bombs on us before we had time to react, and we all might be dead now, instead of heading back to port.

* * *

Glasgow began to feel like a second home. Whenever we had shore leave, Ken and I went there to call on Aileen and Heather. There might have been a shortage of food in Glasgow, but unlike

Halifax there was no shortage of fun, and we didn't want to miss any of it. One night Aileen took me to a dance hall called the Locarno. It had two live bands that performed on a rotating stage so there was never any gap in between sets. One of the bands played Tommy Dorsey numbers, my favourite. Over the next few weeks the Locarno became our special place whenever I had leave. Then as I neared the end of my gunnery course, I was given orders to head back to Halifax. I called on Aileen one last time.

We went to the Locarno as always. We ordered our drinks — soft drinks were the only thing on the menu — and listened as the band kicked into some spirited boogie-woogie music with a heavy backbeat.

Aileen leaned over to me. "All this time we've been going out, Billy O'Connell, and you've never once asked me to dance," she teased. "You're starting to make me feel insecure."

I explained to her that I had never learned how to dance. "My mother's Methodist. Dancing isn't allowed."

"Why not?" Aileen asked.

"They think it leads to more serious sins. Like going to the movies and drinking coffee," I joked.

She laughed and said, "Well, Billy O'Connell,

we can't just sit here all night or we'll grow roots. Up you get."

I protested, but she stood up, took my hand and pulled me onto the dance floor. She was as quick on her feet as she was with her wit.

"You're amazing!" I exclaimed as Aileen skilfully moved to the music.

"Comes from being forced to take Highland dancing when you're seven!" she called to me over the music.

Aileen seemed to float on her feet. Compared to her, I felt like I was lumbering around on snowshoes. But she was such a good dancer that she created the impression that I was leading even when it was her guiding me. I managed to get through it, and in the end, only stepped on her toes twice.

Then the song ended and the band quickly segued into a slow number, "Stardust." I had now gone head-to-head with a German bomber and fired shells big enough to blow a submarine out of the water, but being out on this dance floor made me more nervous. Aileen looked at me expectantly. I could see that she really wanted to dance, and I didn't want to let her down. So I put my arm around her waist and mimicked the movements of the other dancers, who seemed to know what they were doing. I watched the way they swayed to the music and held their partners close, and followed their movements.

After spending so much time inhaling the stench of cordite, paint fumes, bunker oil and the sweat of fifty other sailors, her faint scent of perfume and shampoo gave me a heady feeling. And after sleeping in a wet uniform under a clammy wool blanket, it was exciting to feel her warm, soft skin against mine as her body moved to the music. Soon I forgot how nervous I had been. As we swirled around the dance floor, arms around each other, with the music playing and the happy crowd moving in unison, I discovered that I actually liked dancing — mostly because it gave me a chance to hold Aileen close to me. And for a few brief minutes, I didn't think about submarines or bombers or getting killed.

That night when I walked Aileen home, I told her that my gunnery course was finished and I was being sent back to Halifax.

"Will I see you again, Billy O'Connell?" she asked.

"Of course," I replied. "Greenock is our base on this side of the Atlantic. And it doesn't seem like those German submarines or the war are going away any time soon. So I'll be back."

After that we didn't say anything else about the

war. We didn't want to think about it. But I did make a mental note of where the air raid shelters were, just in case.

But this night was overcast, so there wasn't much chance of the Luftwaffe coming. I walked as slowly as I could, but inevitably we arrived back at Aileen's house. For a few minutes we made small talk, barely above a whisper. Then she said, "I'd better go inside now, before we wake the neighbourhood."

She reached out and squeezed my hand. "Take care of yourself, Billy O'Connell. And you can write to me if you want to."

"I'd like that," I said.

"Just remember, thirty-seven Bell Lane. Like the Scottish-Canadian inventor."

I smiled. Aileen didn't miss a single detail.

A strange feeling passed over me. Standing there on her doorstep, I suddenly missed her already, even though she was right in front of me.

For a brief moment, neither of us knew what to say. Then I leaned in and pressed my lips to hers. She reached up and touched my cheek, then I put my arms around her and drew her close to me. I could feel her hands on my back now, pressing me tightly to her. My heart began pounding so hard, I was afraid she'd be able to hear it.

Then she pulled back just enough to look into

my eyes. “Goodbye, Billy O’Connell,” she whispered. “Safe journeys.”

“Goodbye, Aileen,” I replied. “I’ll write soon.”

She turned and put her key in the front door lock. Our eyes met one last time. She smiled wistfully, then disappeared from view as she closed the door, leaving me alone in the darkened street.

Chapter Six
Mid-June 1941–January 1942

When we arrived at the dock the next morning and saw what was waiting in the harbour for us, Ken and I laughed out loud.

"God almighty," I said, "getting away from the *Wildrose* is harder than scraping gum off your shoe!"

"Yes, back into the old chum bucket for us," Ken muttered.

Now, though, she was at least looking ready for action. On her forward deck was a proper 4-inch gun.

We sailed back to Halifax with a convoy of thirty-six ships, all of them riding high in the water now that they were empty. The trip was almost eerily quiet. Much better than the alternative though. The Germans had just invaded their former ally, the Soviet Union, but we knew that the U-boats would still be out in full force in the North Atlantic. We also knew that HQ in Britain and Halifax had a new weapon, called HuffDuff, that could determine the general location of

German submarines by triangulating their radio signals. That enabled Allied command to guide our convoys away from the direction of the submarine radio transmissions.

But as I knew from stalking deer in the backwoods around Iroquois, a good hunter never lets his prey know he's there. The U-boat crews were stealthy hunters specializing in sudden death, and we had no intention of becoming their prey. So we were constantly vigilant. The ASDIC operators, two at a time, were on duty twenty-four hours a day, listening for a telltale *ping* that told them there was a submarine lurking in the depths. And for every moment of the trip, there was someone in the crow's nest — sometimes me — scanning the water around us all the way to the horizon, on the lookout for a periscope. And my gun crew and I practise fired the 4-inch gun every day to stay sharp. We knew we couldn't always count on technology like HuffDuff to evade the enemy, but on this occasion it worked perfectly and we made it across without a single contact with a German submarine.

* * *

When I got ashore in Halifax I was amazed at how many more new recruits there were on the base, even though we'd only been gone for three months. I was even more surprised to discover that I was now being made an instructor. I had only nine months more experience than my students. But in these desperate times that apparently made me an old salt. And I suppose that compared to the trainees from inland cities like Winnipeg, Saskatoon and Red Deer, I was.

I spent the next few months feeling frustrated about being stuck in Halifax instead of getting in on the action. But there was no arguing with the fact that more instructors were needed to train all the new crews. In North Africa, the Allies were fighting Germany's Afrika Korps, and our forces there and in Malta were in need of constant resupply, so the route from Britain, past Gibraltar and to Africa became an important convoy route, demanding more escort ships and more crews. Ken was assigned to instructor duty too, so at least I had him around to give me his usual running commentary.

There were now so many recruits that even the skating rink or the new barracks couldn't hold them all. Lots of the new recruits I was training grumbled about having to rent space in rooming houses in Halifax. Our guys fumed about landlords renting out rooms for far more than their usual value, taking advantage of the fact that we sailors had nowhere else to go. Some landlords really got them furious by charging half a month's salary for a bedroom that a sailor had to share with three other sailors. There were even stories of some landlords pitting sailor against sailor, auctioning off rooms to the highest bidder. That did nothing to ingratiate the town with us.

After being in Glasgow, Halifax seemed especially dull. Another point of tension was that there were so few places for us sailors to relax when we were ashore. There were still no pubs and few restaurants, and we were discouraged from going into those. There was one bright spot amid the dreariness of Halifax. Dolly McEuen, the wife of a Navy officer, had created the Ajax Club, a place where sailors could have a beer or a soft drink and an inexpensive meal, read, play cards and socialize when we were ashore. Mrs. McEuen had opened it in 1940, and I took full advantage of it over the fall and into the winter of 1941.

Whenever I got a letter from Aileen or my parents, I would head over to the Ajax. There, it was my ritual to settle into an armchair with a Coke, catch up on the news from Iroquois or Glasgow, then write a return letter, which I would post on my way back to the base. It was an oasis of calm and comfort in the middle of a lot of hardship.

On the evening of December 7, 1941, I was sitting in an armchair at the Ajax, having a soft drink and reading a letter from my mom.

Things are really changing around here, she wrote. *A lot of your friends from school have signed up for military service. I ran into Jack Byers down at the post office. He's just joined the Army. He told me to say hi, and that he hopes you're enjoying your "summer vacation," whatever that means.*

Then I remembered that day back in class when Mr. Martin had said that the diplomats would probably negotiate an end to the war and it would be over before summer vacation. I shook my head. It sure hadn't worked out that way. Then I continued reading.

Don and George both got jobs working for the government in Ottawa last month. They're hiring all kinds of people to help run the War Department, clerks and other office workers. The two of them moved into a little flat together there, so with only Burt and Marian left at home now, the place is starting to feel pretty empty. I was just picturing our house like that, half empty, when a sailor ran in from one of the other rooms, shouting, "Guys, you won't believe this! The Japs just bombed Pearl Harbor!"

At first, none of us *did* know whether to believe

it, because as far as we were aware, Japan hadn't even declared war on the United States. But the next day on the radio I heard President Roosevelt say that December 7 was "a date which will live in infamy" as he went on to describe the sneak attack on the U.S. naval base by Japanese aircraft. At the end of his speech he asked Congress to declare war on Japan, and later that same day they did, which in turn prompted the Germans to declare war on the United States.

We had mixed feelings.

It was horrifying to hear of so many thousands of American sailors, guys just like ourselves, being killed and wounded. But on the other hand, America had ten times the population of Canada, and nearly three times that of Great Britain, so having America in the war meant that we had gained a very powerful ally.

"You have to admit, in one way it's a relief," said Ken. "With the Yanks in the war, we'll finally have all their military and industrial clout behind us. Those Krauts won't know what hit 'em!"

As it turned out, in the short term it actually made the war deadlier than ever. German submarines had usually stayed away from North American coastal waters for fear of provoking the United States into declaring war. But now that the United States had joined the Allies, there was no reason for the Germans to avoid sinking ships anywhere they wanted to. And they didn't waste any time getting to work. By January of 1942 they were torpedoing ships up and down the eastern seaboard. The Americans were unready for war and were caught just as flat-footed in the Atlantic as they had been at Pearl Harbor. One German submarine sank a tanker within sight of New York City, and the Americans were so unprepared that not a single U.S. warship was dispatched to counterattack or even investigate. The Germans sank six more ships off the American coast over the next few nights. The U-boats were now almost literally on our doorstep.

Now we had to watch for submarines right off our own coast, not just out in the Atlantic and around Britain. So I wasn't surprised when Ken and I were abruptly reassigned to convoy duty. In truth, I was relieved. I hadn't joined the Navy to become a "barrack stanchion." I wanted to sink some German submarines and wipe that smug look off Hitler's face just as much as I ever did. And now that I'd be on convoy duty again, I'd have a chance to see Aileen.

Chapter Seven
January 1942

As we left Halifax Harbour to form up the convoy, the weather was fair. The water was bitingly cold, but the seas were calm and the skies clear. Normally, calm seas and clear skies were the answer to a sailor's prayers in a North Atlantic winter, but in wartime it was the worst situation you could imagine, because it was easier for the U-boats to operate. For the first few days of the trip we had air cover from the Royal Canadian Air Force. Subs were so fearful of air attacks that they would dive at the first sign of a plane. On this occasion we were kept company by an RCAF Digby bomber, which provided plenty of deterrent, riding shotgun out ahead of the convoy. Unfortunately, none of our aircraft had the range to provide protection for us all the way. About 600 miles east of Newfoundland, as Ken and I stood watch on the forward gun deck, the Digby reached the outer edge of its operational range. It banked and doubled back toward us, wagging its wings in farewell as it flew over our deck and back toward its base in Newfoundland.

"Well, there goes our big friend," Ken muttered. "It's into the Black Pit with us."

We had now entered what was officially known as the mid-Atlantic Air Gap. But the Black Pit is what we called it, and that's exactly what it felt like when we were sailing into it.

"Six hundred miles of open ocean to cross, with no air protection. It's just us against the U-boats now," muttered Ken as he cleaned the salt off the Lewis gun.

One of the petty officers, a guy by the name of Jenkins who had been reassigned to our ship for this leg, added, "I've just come off a westbound run. The Black Pit is crawling with subs now. They've figured out the range of our escort aircraft almost to the mile. So they've been massing their wolf packs out there in the Gap, where they can hit us hardest without worrying about our bombers getting the drop on them."

"I'll check the four-inch gun," I said. "Sounds like we might need it."

Later that afternoon after inspecting the gun, I spent an hour up in the crow's nest. The sea was calm. The sunset was red and gold, the last rays glinting silver off the gentle wavetops. By the time I was about to go off duty, the ocean and the sky above it had grown dark. The moon hadn't risen yet, so we were sailing in near complete darkness. I was thinking that for once the sea was gentle enough that my clothes weren't wet, my hammock wasn't wet, the mess deck wasn't wet, and I might actually get four luxuriously dry hours of sleep without being flung about like a rag doll.

I was on the gun deck when I heard a voice from the ASDIC room behind me.

"Incoming torpedoes!" shouted the ASDIC operator. "Sounds like a freight train! They're coming straight at us from the stern, off to port side!"

Without a moment's hesitation the captain called out, "Hard to starboard!"

The bow swung round and the ship leaned over at a crazy angle. I hung on to my 4-inch gun to keep from getting thrown overboard. From my position I could see two trails of bubbles racing toward us from out of the dark, frigid water. Beyond that, there was just the blackness of a North Atlantic night.

After months of preparing and waiting, I finally had my first encounter with a U-boat. And now, as I watched the torpedo trails homing in on us and felt the ship turning agonizingly slowly as the helmsman threw the wheel around, I wondered if it would be my last.

I looked past the trails from the torpedoes, out

over the ocean, but saw nothing but blackness.

"Star shell!" I ordered.

Quickly the gun crew opened the breech and loaded it in, along with a bag of cordite explosive to propel it, and the firing plug to ignite the cordite. I calculated the upward angle of the gun barrel, then gave the order.

"Fire!"

There was a deep rumble, then the star shell exploded a thousand yards in the air, a mile to stern. We'd gotten lucky. Beneath the sudden explosion of brilliant white light, less than a thousand yards behind us, I saw the silhouette of a submarine's conning tower and German sailors scrambling back inside as the submarine was already beginning an emergency crash-dive. The torpedoes hurtled past our stern, missing us by only a few yards. Ken opened up on the sub with the Lewis gun. But we were too far away. His bullets splashed into the ocean just short of the sub. I'd gotten lucky with the star shell, but time was working against us. A U-boat could crash-dive in less than thirty seconds, and they'd begun to submerge the moment the star shell exploded above them.

"I need a high-explosive shell!" I called out while we were still turning. As the gun crew loaded it in I could see the conning tower almost fully submerged. The torpedoes hurtled past us, just missing our stern. The burning magnesium from the star shell was still slowly, gently falling, so close to the waves that its light was reflecting back up into the sky. I had a clear view, calm seas and a good idea of the sub's range. My crew was fast, but the old-fashioned manual breech-loading gun on our corvette was painfully slow. The crew slammed the shell in, then the bag of cordite. By now the periscope was slipping beneath the water. I decided to take the shot anyway.

"Fire!" I shouted. A couple of seconds later the shell slammed into the waves directly above where the U-boat had been, sending up a frothing column of water.

It was a clean shot, dead-on where the submarine had been. Five seconds sooner and I would have blown that U-boat into next week. But it came too late. The submarine had escaped.

It reminded me of times when I was a kid, out on the St. Lawrence, and a fish would nibble the bait right off the hook, then escape. Only there was so much more at stake now.

"Damn!" I muttered, holding back my urge to shout a torrent of swear words. I had been so close to sinking that sub.

Our captain wasn't giving up though. Slow as

the corvette was, we could still close that gap in less than two minutes. The depth-charge crews got ready to fire. But of course the German submariners weren't going to make it easy for us by sitting there waiting. Their subs could only go 7 knots when submerged, but even so they could have gone hundreds of yards in any direction, unseen, by the time we got to their last known position, not to mention up to 200 yards or more straight down. We had to land a depth charge no more than 5 yards from them to make a kill.

"Contact!" shouted the ASDIC operator.

"Drop depth charges!" shouted the captain.

We dropped two patterns of 300-pound depth charges. The explosions from each one sent a shock wave of water churning up into the night sky. But it was apparently without result.

There was a pause after the explosions. Everything was silent except for the thrumming of the engines.

"Contact lost," came the response relayed from the ASDIC cabin.

"Maybe we sank 'em!" an eager voice called out in the dark.

But minutes later there was no sign of debris or an oil slick to indicate that we'd hit the German sub, so we assumed it had survived. We sailed patterns through the area for another half an hour without picking up anything on the ASDIC.

The last of the convoy was by now disappearing over the horizon, so we were ordered to call off the search and rejoin the other ships. If not, there was a very real danger that the U-boat could slip between us and the merchant ships, and if we straggled too far behind, we couldn't protect them from another attack.

I silently cursed Mackenzie King, the cheap bastard, living in his dream world, betting against all odds that war wouldn't come — and that if it did, it could somehow be fought with hand-me-down equipment from the First World War. With a modern gun I could have gotten in the one critical shot that would have sent the U-boat straight down to Davy Jones' locker. Instead, it had survived to kill Allied seamen and sink ships and their precious cargoes that so many people had put their blood, sweat and tears into, and that so many people were counting on both to survive and to take the fight to the enemy.

As we steamed toward the convoy I went off watch and down to my hammock. It was dry, and under any other circumstances I would have slept beautifully. But knowing that a U-boat was still out there, I had a hard time winding down.

The next morning the sun rose over another calm sea. The clouds were lit up golden and pink. It could have been a beautiful day on Lake Superior. But it wasn't. It was a beautiful day in the Black Pit, so no matter how pleasant it looked, death was awaiting us at any moment.

All day long the convoy steamed ahead, and our ASDIC, as well as the radar that had been recently fitted, picked up nothing. Then again, neither had they picked up the submarine that almost sank us the night before. So I wasn't feeling especially confident. From the gun positions and the crow's nest, we scanned the horizon and all the water in between, looking for a surfaced submarine or a periscope. And all day long, all we saw was water. But we knew the U-boats were out there somewhere. After last night's contact it was only a question of when and where they'd choose to strike.

The answer came not long after the winter sun set over the western horizon, and the darkness closed in around us. We were at the rear of the convoy, sailing a zigzag pattern to present a more difficult target, when I saw a flash of light in the sky about 2 miles ahead of us. A moment later there was another flash. It was followed by a rumble like heavy thunder — the sound of German torpedoes slamming into one of our merchant ships. Within moments flames licked skyward.

The alarm bell rang.

"Action stations!" called the cox'n.

We immediately accelerated to full speed. The ship that had been hit was on the starboard side of the convoy, on the outside edge of the front row — a position the crews called the coffin corner, because those ships often got torpedoed first.

Silhouetted by flames from burning bunker oil floating on the water, the merchant ship listed heavily. I scanned the sea for any sight of a submarine. When I looked back toward the torpedoed freighter, the only thing still showing was the stern, then it too slid under the waves.

Meanwhile the entire convoy behind it kept right on going, past where the freighter had gone down. We weren't allowed to stop when the convoy was under attack. Those were the rules. If we had, it would have just made us sitting ducks and let the enemy escape. On the port side of the convoy another burst of flames shot into the sky, so high that I could see the red and orange reflecting off the clouds above us. An oil tanker. It ignited with a series of explosions so massive the shock waves rattled our rigging.

Now, in the centre of the convoy, another

merchantman exploded. That meant a U-boat had penetrated the formation and was running at periscope depth between the columns, attacking our ships while making it almost impossible for us to counterattack, because our own merchant ships were in the way. The U-boat I'd scared off with the star shell the previous night must have been keeping its distance but tracking us the whole time, sending our position on to other submarines that were now lying in wait. I was madder than ever about the ancient 4-inch gun I had to use.

But there was no time for that because seconds later an alarm sounded.

The *Wildrose* came about hard to port. Then the depth-charge crew began rolling charges off the rails at the back of the ship. Our ship rattled as each of them exploded. An oil slick stained the surface, but the captain judged that it wasn't enough to indicate a kill. We had probably just given them a good shaking up. The enemy hadn't been vanquished, just chased away. And that was cold comfort. Because we were up against a relentless opponent, and we knew that even if we drove them off tonight, they'd be back again tomorrow.

As we got close to where the first freighter had been attacked, a hellish vision emerged out of the night in front of us. Burning fuel oil floated on the water, the pulsating yellow light illuminating the faces of the survivors of a torpedoed freighter.

I heard their cries for help and felt sick that we couldn't do a thing for them. Worse, as they bobbed helplessly in the icy ocean, a destroyer plowed right through them.

"Isn't there anything we can do for them?" asked an ordinary seaman. He was baby-faced, probably new to the war, a tortured expression on his face.

"Not a damned thing," I replied, "at least not yet."

"Just doesn't seem right," he said.

"I know it doesn't," I replied. "But if we stop and give the Krauts a target, they'll open us up like a can of tomatoes."

The young seaman peered into the dark, hands gripping the railing, that tortured look on his face as we heard the moans, the cries for help, then the inevitable explosions of our depth charges — with fewer and fewer voices calling for help after each detonation.

It was horrifying to see, but it was no accident. When a combat ship made contact with an enemy U-boat, it was automatically under strict orders to press home the attack and try to sink the submarine. A commander could be court-martialled for disobeying that protocol. We knew it and so did the merchant sailors in the water. We had all received the same training: if we were ever unfortunate enough to find ourselves bobbing around in the ocean when our own ships were engaged in a depth-charge attack nearby, we didn't expect help. Our own ships weren't even *allowed* to help us. Instead, when we saw the explosives drop into the water, we were supposed to cover our mouths with one hand and our butts with the other. If we didn't, and the depth charge exploded underneath us, the surge of water could literally blast upward through the anus and blow our guts out of our mouths.

Plumes of spray shot up into the sky where the depth charges were exploding. There were men everywhere in the water, screaming in fear and agony. Every instinct told me to help them. But until the attack was called off, there was nothing that I or anybody else could do.

Finally, when all of the escorts had lost ASDIC contact with the U-boats for more than half an hour, the area was assumed to be clear of them. There was no hope of us sinking any of the submarines now — and, we hoped, no chance of being torpedoed. So we and another escort ship finally set about picking up the survivors while the rest of the convoy and the escorts steamed on. The convoy never stopped for anything. It had to make it through no matter what.

We dropped scramble nets over the side of the ship and picked up the survivors as quickly as we could. We had never done this before except in drills. The reality was a lot grimmer than what we'd seen in practice. By now some of the men had been clinging to debris in the freezing water for a long time, and their hands were so numb they couldn't hold on to the nets. Others were so badly injured that they didn't have the strength to pull themselves out of the water. So the captain ordered a lifeboat to be lowered, and we began hauling the survivors out.

I had to remain at my gun station. We ran without lights, so I could barely make out the shadowy figures in the water. Some were calling out for help. But others, many others, were bobbing lifelessly, killed either by burns, exposure to the icy water or by our own depth charges. They were covered in thick, black bunker oil and looked just like the sailors I'd seen in the newsreel up in Port Arthur right before I joined the Navy. It was all reality now. And I felt sick.

When I came off watch, I saw several merchant

seamen huddled under blankets in the forward mess decks. They were Norwegian and none of them spoke any English. There was another man on the mess table just underneath my hammock. He must have been among the worst, because they had to lie him down.

We didn't have a doctor on board. Our ship was too small for that. We just had a tiny sick bay where one of the crewmen who had been trained as a medic gave the most basic medical care. The injured man seemed to be in his early fifties, but it was hard to tell. His face was burned pretty badly. His skin, hair and clothes were covered in black bunker oil as thick as molasses. Older guys like him didn't have the physical stamina to easily survive such an ordeal. We got as much of the oil off him as we could, and our medic gave him some painkillers and disinfected his wounds, then wrapped him in heavy blankets.

The next morning when it was light enough, we transferred the survivors to a merchant ship, since they had far more room to spare than our corvette, which was already crammed with men, ammunition and food. Only the wounded merchant sailor on the mess table stayed behind, since he was too badly injured to be moved. The hope was to keep him alive long enough to get him to port, so he could be taken to hospital and get proper care.

He lay on the table for another two days. From time to time he moaned in pain, but otherwise remained unconscious. Once, during the night, I heard him mumbling excitedly. I thought he was coming round. But when I looked over the edge of my hammock, I saw that even though his lips were moving, his eyes were closed.

There was nothing I or anybody else on the ship could do for him, so I went back to sleep. When I got out of my hammock to start my morning watch a couple of hours later, his eyes were open, looking almost straight up at me. But they were glassy and lifeless. I put my finger on his wrist to check his pulse. His skin was cold and he had no heartbeat.

I found Petty Officer Jenkins. "That Norwegian merchantman. He didn't make it," I said.

"Okay, I'll tell the captain," was all Jenkins said.

We buried the dead sailor at sea later that morning. The shipwright sewed the man inside a canvas sheet, along with some heavy brass practice shell casings so he would sink quickly.

I was part of the detail that carried his corpse to the railing. The captain read a brief prayer. A few of the crewmen stood watch, keeping their eyes peeled for a periscope to make sure we weren't about to be attacked. Then we slowed down just long enough to let the dead sailor slip into the water with some dignity. We were still in the Black Pit and couldn't risk becoming a sitting duck for a German torpedo.

I heard the captain say, "We therefore commit his body to the deep," and then the enshrouded corpse was released into the ocean. With the weight of the shell casings, the body plunged feet first into the water, barely making a splash as it hit the surface. The ocean always seemed dark and opaque, even during the day. I had never seen a burial at sea before, and I was surprised to notice that the white canvas shroud was visible beneath the water for a fathom or so as it sank, until it slipped away, disappearing into the vast emptiness of the North Atlantic.

It left me with a leaden feeling to think that a man's life could be taken away so easily, and swallowed up so completely. Later one of the junior crew brought our lunch to the mess table, but I couldn't eat. I kept picturing that dying sailor lying on the table, moaning in misery, far from home and loved ones. I couldn't eat at that table again for the rest of the voyage.

That afternoon word went around that we were out of the Black Pit. An hour or so later the distinctive drone of the four engines of a Short Sunderland flying boat told me we had air cover again. It was no guarantee of safety, but it tilted the odds in our favour. And for now, that was enough.

Chapter Eight
January 1942

After we had escorted the remaining ships safely across, Ken and I took the train into Glasgow. But we didn't immediately go to visit Aileen and Heather. Having witnessed so much death so close up for the first time in my life, I needed to sort out my feelings before I could be myself again. I didn't want Aileen to see me like this.

"I know what we need, O'Connell," said Ken. "I've heard that these pubs are fun places. Let's go have a look."

In Iroquois there was something disreputable about the notion of a place where people got together and drank. "My mother always said that fire and brimstone would be my fate if I ever set foot in a bar," I said.

Ken gave me a pained look.

"But I figure it's too late for that," I continued. "Might as well find out what all the fuss is about."

"Amen to that," said Ken with a grin.

We found a pub called the Crown and Thistle and entered. It was warm and bright inside, with dark polished wood, frosted glass and shiny brass fittings.

There were all kinds of people there: children drinking sodas and playing darts, ladies in their seventies nursing drinks that I later found out were gin and tonics.

"So, O'Connell," said Ken, "does this look like the satanic den of sin that your mother warned you about?"

"Not exactly," I answered. "I have to admit that those old ladies with the blue-rinsed hair are a bit of a surprise. Strangest looking demons I've ever seen."

Besides the children and old people, there were Royal Navy sailors, a few Air Force personnel and several soldiers too, mixed in among the crowd of factory workers and other civilians. Everybody was just chatting and having some laughs.

We were quickly welcomed by the regulars with greetings of "Hello, Canada. What's your pleasure?" Soon Ken and I had a couple of pints of reddy-brown Scottish ale in front of us. I took a sip. It was smooth and malty, and quite delicious.

People kept coming up to us and asking about Canada, wondering whether we knew their Uncle Angus in Saskatchewan, if people really lived in igloos, and what it was like on convoy duty. I spoke to a Royal Navy petty officer who sailed the convoy run to Russia through the Arctic Ocean in the worst winter storm conditions imaginable. I met a guy named Charlie who was a bomb aimer on a Royal Air Force Wellington. He'd flown missions into the heart of the Nazi Reich, over Berlin and Hamburg.

"The German flak is so heavy over those cities, you feel like you could get out of the plane and walk on it," Charlie said. He described seeing British bombers explode in mid-air 3 miles above a burning city after taking direct hits from the anti-aircraft flak, bursting into fireballs before their crews even had a chance to bail out.

And I met a Scottish artillery officer named Craig whose unit had been tasked with fighting a rearguard action to slow the German advance during the Allied retreat in the Battle of France. "It came down to a vicious street battle in a town just outside Dunkirk," said Craig. "We went head-to-head against the elite of the Panzer tank corps. We were only a few hundred feet apart the whole time, for an entire day. Our guns and their guns, pounding the crap out of each other till the town was reduced to rubble all around us."

I was still working on my first pint, but noticed that his glass was empty, so I bought him another round.

"Ta," said Craig with a nod to me as the barman placed his ale in front of him.

"What happened?" asked Ken.

Craig had a faraway look in his eyes, like he was watching the battle as he described it to us. "We fought them to a standstill. Kept at it until we ran out of ammunition and had to take to our heels. We left our heavy weapons behind and got the hell out of there just ahead of the Hun as the last boats departed for England. Lost a lot of good men that day, and I've still got a couple of chunks of shrapnel in me. One in my shoulder and one in my arse," he said, laughing as he pointed out their approximate locations. "But they say that we slowed the Germans down enough that it enabled thousands of our fellows to get off the beach and into the boats to fight the Krauts another day in North Africa, instead of spending the rest of the war in a prisoner-of-war camp."

Ken and I talked so much with Charlie and Craig and so many other people that by the end of the evening my throat was hoarse. But it was good. I felt better, and it wasn't just the two pints of dark Scottish ale I'd had by the end of the night. Being able to tell aloud the things I had seen, to other people who understood what I'd gone through because they'd had similar experiences, was a huge weight off my shoulders.

Ken and I left the pub and found our way to the Salvation Army, where we bedded down for the night. I fell into a blissful eight hours of uninterrupted sleep.

* * *

The next day I made my way to 37 Bell Lane and tapped the door knocker. I heard small footsteps running for the door, and a moment later was greeted by a red-haired boy with a gap-toothed grin.

I said hello, to which he responded, "Are you that Canadian, then?"

"I'm not sure," I replied. "I'm *a* Canadian. Just not sure if I'm *that* Canadian."

"Oh, you're that Canadian all right," he said, with a smaller version of Aileen's grin.

A moment later a middle-aged woman with a pleasant face came to the door.

"Hello, I'm Bill O'Connell," I said, holding out my hand.

She smiled at me. "I'm Mrs. Henderson, Aileen's mother. And mother to this one too. Say hello properly then, Jimmy."

"Hello," said Jimmy as he shyly held out his hand.

I shook it, then pointed behind his ear.

"What's that growing behind your ear?" I asked.

"What?" he asked, wide-eyed.

I reached behind his ear, gave my wrist a flick and out popped the Hershey chocolate bar I'd put aside for the occasion.

"There it is!" I said.

"Mom, did you see that?" he asked. "I had a chocolate bar growing behind my ear!"

"Say thank you," said Mrs. Henderson.

"But Mom, it was growing behind my *ear*!" he shrieked.

"That's very lovely, but say thank you anyway to Mr. O'Connell for finding it for you."

"Thank you!" came the singsong reply.

Then Mrs. Henderson explained that the munitions factory was operating round-the-clock shifts, seven days a week, so even though this was a Saturday, Aileen was working. Mr. Henderson was upstairs sleeping, because he worked night shifts as a machinist.

"But Aileen will be home and washed up by six-thirty," said Mrs. Henderson. "We'd be pleased to have you for dinner if you'd like to come back."

"Thank you," I replied. "I'd like that very much."

I spent the rest of the day exploring Glasgow on

my own. When I returned that evening, Aileen's father greeted me at the door and introduced himself as Ewan. He had a strong handshake and an easy smile. He told me that he had served in the Royal Navy during the First World War, twenty-five years earlier.

"I got my first combat experience at the Battle of Jutland," he said. "That was a nasty bit of business."

He was understating it. The Battle of Jutland was infamous. More than six thousand British, Canadian and Australian sailors had died in that battle between the Royal Navy and the German fleet.

"But you lads have got it just as tough on convoy duty," he said. "And we're grateful to you for it. I reckon half the food on this table is here because of you fellows making sure the Jerry submarines didn't feed it all to the fish."

He looked like he was about to say something else when Mrs. Henderson smiled at him. "We are indeed grateful. But I'm sure young Bill here would like a break from the war, so let's talk about something else, shall we?"

Mr. Henderson paused, like he was deciding whether to argue the point. Then he smiled at her. "So, tell us about Canada then. Are you all as rich as the Yanks?" he asked me. Now I knew where Aileen got her sense of humour.

"No. We don't all drive around in Cadillacs and have servants, like the people you see in the American films." I told him that we even hunted and fished for our dinner during the worst of the Depression.

"Oh, you really are well off then," Mr. Henderson joked. "Here it's only the royal family and the lords and barons and all those sorts of mucky-mucks who get to run around shooting at their supper."

As for the Hendersons' dinner, it was a lamb stew which, given the rationing, consisted of a few very small pieces of lamb surrounded by a sea of gravy, potatoes, carrots, turnips and onions. But I didn't care. It felt like being at home again, and the Hendersons' small row house was like a mansion after being crammed into the mess deck of the *Wildrose* for nearly the past two weeks.

Later, I thanked her parents for dinner, then Aileen and I went to the Locarno. This time I moved much more confidently about the dance floor, and the horrors of the sea battle at last felt far away.

Chapter Nine
February–March 1942

The return journey to Halifax was my first real taste of a North Atlantic winter. For the first portion, from Scotland out above Northern Ireland, it was almost balmy because of the Gulf Stream's warm current. But as we sailed south of Iceland toward Greenland and into the cold water below the Arctic Circle, the Gulf Stream's influence diminished and the weather changed abruptly. At first I just noticed the chill in the air and that I could now see my breath. Then the waves grew bigger, the troughs between them became deeper. At last the air and the water grew so cold that when spray from the waves hit the ship, it instantly froze onto every metal surface.

Off watch, a bunch of us lay in our swaying hammocks and tried to sleep. But we could feel the waves growing higher as the ship pitched and rocked, and the hammocks swaying more and more. "Why the hell don't they steer us away from this?" muttered one of the guys.

A petty officer who happened to be passing

through said, "I'll tell you why. Because we got a warning that there's a huge wolf pack on the prowl four hundred nautical miles south of here, below the weather front."

Our more northerly route kept us away from those subs, but it put us into the teeth of a vicious winter storm. We had entered the Black Pit once again, and the brass evidently felt that without air cover, the threat of massed U-boats was so dire that the treacherous weather was the lesser of two evils. And crazy as it sounds, it was true. When the waves were 60 feet high the U-boats couldn't fire their torpedoes accurately, so they usually avoided these weather systems completely.

That was small comfort as the gale raged around us now. The cold, stormy weather made life absolutely miserable, and the fact that the Navy still hadn't issued proper winter clothing added to our discomfort. We had only our wool uniforms, with oilskins over them, along with cheap non-issue sweaters that we'd picked up ashore.

As we sailed north into the teeth of an Arctic winter, the problem of inadequate clothing became much less serious than the danger from the ice that was constantly forming on the upper surfaces of our ship. It built up on everything, in layers as thick as my wrist. It was potentially as deadly as a torpedo or a bomb. The guns would get so thickly covered in ice that if we didn't chip it off, they couldn't be aimed or fired. The lifeboats became frozen uselessly to the ship. One night a young stoker on only his second voyage slipped on the icy deck and went over the side. We never saw him again.

We had been warned that ice could also collect on the upper surfaces and make a ship so heavy that it would capsize or sink. I found out how true that was one day when I was on watch and saw a Greek freighter, heavily sheathed in ice, ride to the top of a 60-foot wave. As the freighter crested the massive wave it plunged nose-first down the other side at a steep angle, then into the water at the bottom of the trough . . . and simply didn't come up again.

"Merchantman down!" I shouted. The alarm was passed through the raging wind from crewman to crewman till it reached the wheelhouse.

The captain ordered us to pull out of formation and search. Plowing through the towering waves, we circled the area for fifteen minutes looking for survivors. But nothing came to the surface, not so much as a life jacket or a scrap of wood. The sea had swallowed that freighter whole.

After that, despite being pelted by sleet that felt

like icy razors tearing the skin right off our faces, all of us — from the captain on down to the lowliest stoker — were out on deck every spare minute we had, knocking the ice off. We went at it with everything we could lay our hands on: hammers, axe handles, crowbars, wrenches and pipes. It didn't matter how many times we slipped and fell on the oily, icy deck, or how numb our fingers got from the spray and sleet, we kept at it until we just couldn't smash any more ice. Then the next guy would take over.

All around us, the storm kept blowing harder. The waves were now the height of a six-storey office building. Normally we were only seasick for the first three or four days after being on the water, but the ocean was so violent that we were constantly vomiting. Guys threw up over the side, but it would get blown back by the wind or carried by the waves back onto the ship, so we'd be chipping that off along with the ice. It was a miserable job, but I figured that if the weather was so terrible that we found ourselves chipping frozen puke off our own ship, it was definitely too rough for the U-boats to attack.

One evening, with the worst storm conditions yet, the north wind was screaming through the rigging as I finished my watch. My face and hands were numb and my ears were ringing from the near-hurricane-force gusts. I crawled into my hammock in my cold, sodden uniform, pulled the clammy wool blankets over myself and tried to sleep. The mess was as frigid as a meat locker. Our breath turned to frost on the steel ceiling. Icy water from the upper decks dripped down into my hammock, so I pulled my oilskin over my head and blankets to make a little tent to protect myself. I was exhausted, but could only fall into a sort of half sleep, because the ship was pitching and rolling even more violently now than when I had been on watch. Ankle-deep water formed a lake beneath my hammock, sloshing around, mimicking the motion of the ocean outside.

"God, this is like trying to fall asleep on a roller coaster," Ken muttered.

"Yeah, while wearing cold, wet clothing and inhaling the stink of paint, bunker oil, sweat, stale breath and puke," I answered.

The waves became so high I was almost pitched face first out of the hammock. The corvette was rolling further and further on its side as it crested each wave. Each time it took longer to right itself. Finally one wave crashed into us so hard that the water came pouring into the mess deck, hundreds of gallons all at once.

As I swung in my hammock the whole room tilted around me and just seemed to stay there, so when I looked up I could see the wall. I thought we'd been knocked over on our side and I hung on while I waited for the next big wave to turn us over completely. In the dim light I couldn't tell who was awake and who was asleep, but nobody said a word. There was no shouting, no crying. Everyone was silent. I resigned myself to the fact that I was probably going to die tonight. It was that simple. But slowly I saw the line of the ceiling begin to right itself again and become parallel to my line of vision. Then we hit the next wave and the ship tilted again, though not quite as much as the time before. I began to relax a bit, trying to convince myself that the worst of it was over. At last I fell asleep. Not a very deep sleep, but enough that I wouldn't be completely stunned when I went on watch in a few hours' time.

I awoke to a voice announcing, "We're out of the Black Pit!" When I opened my eyes I could tell from the rocking of the ship that the storm had died down, at least a bit. If we were out of the Black Pit, it meant that we had air cover once again — and a much better chance of staying alive. But the convoy had been scattered by the storm. It took us more than two days to regroup.

Only then could we fully assess the damage.

The lead ship, a destroyer much larger and more powerful than us, had suffered such severe damage that it had to put into port at St. John's for repairs. Its wheelhouse had been torn off by the storm and blown right into the ocean. On another ship the thick bulkheads had started to warp from the constant battering of the waves.

Our little corvette had suffered much less damage. My feeling about her began to change. She was cold, wet, crowded and slow, and I still didn't like any of those things. But now I knew that the *Wildrose* was tough and reliable and she could get us safely through the worst that the North Atlantic could throw at her.

When our convoy arrived in Halifax we were all given two weeks' leave to recuperate, since it had been such a gruelling round trip. I was exhausted, but thrilled by the news.

Two weeks was just enough time to go visit my family in Iroquois. Despite the storms and the U-boats, one advantage to being in the Navy was that we had to come back to Canada regularly, so on occasion we were able to visit our families, something the Army and Air Force fellows never got to do once they were overseas. I'd never got the chance yet, so I wasted no time in going to the station on Hollis Street. My mom had mentioned in a recent letter that they had a telephone now, so I called my parents to let them know I was coming. Then I bought a ticket for the next train home.

Late in the afternoon the following day I got off at the station in Iroquois. It wasn't a long walk from there to home. I smoothed out the creases in my uniform, then slung my kit bag over my shoulder and set out. I had only walked a couple of blocks when I ran into Mr. Martin, my history teacher, in front of the post office.

"Bill O'Connell," he said, slowing down and shaking my hand. "You don't look like the skinny kid who used to sit in my class charming all the girls." I didn't remember ever having done that. I figured it was his stock line. "How is the Navy treating you?" he asked.

"As good as it can, I guess," I answered. "We were badly unprepared at the start. But I think we're starting to make some headway."

He smiled, sort of sadly. "I remember telling you a couple of years ago that the diplomats were probably working behind the scenes and the war would be over by the time you went on summer vacation."

"I remember that too," I replied.

There was an awkward pause. He looked serious.

"I was in the first war, you know. Served in the Artillery Corps in France."

"I never knew that," I said.

"That's because I never told any of you students," he replied. "Never told most people after I came home. Didn't want to talk about it. I saw things over there that I wish I could forget. But I never will. I guess I hoped the politicians were too smart to ever put us through that kind of misery ever again. But I was wrong."

"Nearly everybody was wrong, Mr. Martin," I said.

I had always thought of him as just a boring guy with a boring job who didn't know what he was talking about, thinking the war would be over by summer vacation.

"You look like you're either coming or going," he said, motioning to my kit bag. "Which is it?"

"Coming," I replied. "Just got off leave from convoy duty."

"Well, I don't want to keep you from seeing your family. You'll be back in the thick of it soon enough." He reached out and shook my hand again. "Good seeing you," he said. "Be safe. And give those bastards hell."

"Thanks, Mr. Martin," I said. "I'll try."

I had never heard him swear before. He wasn't

talking to me like a teacher to a kid anymore, but as a soldier to a soldier.

I turned away and continued toward my parents' house, which was just a couple of blocks away. Little boys saluted me as I walked down the main street, some very excited, others looking extremely serious, standing at attention. I tried to maintain what I thought was a dignified military bearing as I walked through the town, but by the time I reached the end of my street I was so excited to see my family that I was almost running.

I knocked on the door, then opened it. "It's me, Bill!" I called out. By happy coincidence, it was almost dinnertime, and the moment I entered the house I could smell the welcoming, familiar aroma of my mother's home cooking.

I heard footsteps racing down the hallway. "Mom, Dad, it's Billy!" I heard Marian call out. Then she and Burt came charging around the corner into the front hall. They threw themselves into my arms and I hugged them tightly. It had been nearly a year and a half since I'd last seen them, and I was surprised how much taller they both were.

My mother and father came out of the parlour, smiling. My mother kissed me; my dad shook my hand, then put his arms around me.

"Look at you," he said. "You've grown into a

man. What do they feed you in the Navy?"

I guess Burt and Marian weren't the only ones who had gotten bigger. "You wouldn't want to know, Dad," I replied. "The food in port is okay, but out at sea? Well, let's just say we do a lot better at home with Mom's cooking. Trust me!"

My mother smiled. After the many barely edible meals I'd eaten aboard corvettes, I had a new appreciation for what a good job Mom had accomplished, feeding us with limited resources throughout the Depression.

We had supper together in the dining room, with a tablecloth, placemats and the best napkins, something she normally only ever used when we had guests for dinner. We had a roast chicken, one of the birds from the coop that my parents kept in the backyard. They grew beautiful beans and tomatoes in their garden too, but it was winter, so we just had root vegetables from last season that they had stored in the cold cellar: potatoes, carrots and turnips. They were delicious. I hadn't had such a good meal since I'd gone to Aileen's home for dinner. We didn't talk about the war that first night. Just about the news in Iroquois and the weather that winter, and I told them about Halifax, and Glasgow and Aileen. My parents smiled a little to each other when I mentioned her.

The next day, when Marian and Burt were finished school, I took them out shopping on Iroquois's small main street. We went to Beamish, our modest version of a department store. I told Marian and Burt to pick out whatever they wanted. After the long years of the Depression, and the constant, grinding deprivation that made my parents very thrifty, it gave Marian and Burt both a thrill to be able to buy something without thinking about the cost. And it gave me a thrill to indulge them. Marian chose some hair ribbons and a little bathtub filled with dolls. Burt picked out a model ship.

As for Iroquois, the main street seemed even sleepier than before the war. In fact, it was a bit of a ghost town. I went by Jack's place, but his mom told me that he'd already shipped out to Camp Borden, where he was training in the Canadian Armoured Corps. Most of the other guys I'd known in school were either off fighting in the war, or had moved to Toronto or Montreal to work in armaments factories. Many of the girls I'd known, as well as the guys who, like Don and George, couldn't pass the military physical, had moved to Ottawa to work in the federal civil service, which was growing rapidly because of the war.

After the bustle of places like Halifax, Greenock

and Glasgow, Iroquois was pretty dull, though I didn't tell my family that. I kept myself busy doing chores, like feeding the chickens and collecting eggs. But the henhouse out back had become more or less a hobby for my family, because like me, my older brothers were sending money home, and my dad's job was steady, so the financial pressure on my folks had eased up a lot.

Much as I loved seeing my parents and brother and sister, there was nothing for me to really do in Iroquois. It felt like I was in a sort of limbo. Because my dad had never served in the military, he wasn't able to understand what I was going through. I didn't want my parents to worry, so I didn't tell them about the horrors I'd seen.

One night when my mom and Burt and Marian weren't around, Dad quietly asked me, "What's it like out there on the ocean? From what I hear, it sounds pretty dangerous." I hesitated, unsure how to answer him. He continued. "Some of the lake freighter captains say there are even German submarines out in the St. Lawrence now, up past Quebec City."

He had heard right. At least the rumours. But I didn't want him to worry.

"That's just talk, Dad." I said. "There might be the odd submarine that goes off course, but with all the air cover we have, the Germans would be crazy to spend much time in the St. Lawrence. And when there are corvettes around, the U-boats hightail it," I lied, "because they know if they get anywhere near us, we'll blow them out of the water."

My dad smiled. I think he believed me. Or wanted to. So he didn't press the point.

But I knew my comrades on other ships were out battling the submarines, and I knew I was needed there too. I didn't feel particularly useful hanging around Iroquois, so when it was time to return to base, I was actually a little relieved.

Chapter Ten
March 1942–February 1943

When I returned to duty, the worst of the winter storms had passed. Crew members were constantly being transferred between ships, and I was sorry to discover when I got to the barracks in Halifax that Ken was gone. He'd been assigned to destroyer duty. I found out that he was being trained on a new type of gun called a Bofors, a devastating new anti-aircraft weapon. Lucky dog, I thought. I envied Ken the chance to train on something powerful and brand new, instead of being stuck on the *Wildrose* with antique weapons.

Despite the shortcomings of some of our equipment, we were gaining experience we had lacked at the beginning of the war. More and more of our ships were now equipped with radar, so we could detect surfaced submarines during the long winter nights or when it was foggy, which was a lot of the time.

On top of that, our commanders changed the way we operated. Instead of working solo, our ships were organized into co-ordinated escort groups, using our ASDIC and radar to seek out U-boats and then working collectively to destroy them. Gradually we started to give the Germans as good as we got, and the tally of German submarines destroyed by Allied forces began to grow.

German bombers were still taking their toll on us as well. We were especially afraid of the Focke-Wulf 200 Kurier. Originally built as a commercial plane to fly passengers from Europe to North America, its long operational radius gave it the ability to bomb convoys as far out as Iceland. Since our fighter planes lacked the range to square off against them over the Atlantic to counter that threat, the British built CAM ships — merchant vessels with one catapult-launched Hawker Hurricane fighter on each. It was a peculiar looking arrangement that I saw used in action only once. As we were passing east of Iceland, the radar picked up an incoming German bomber. The Hurricane was catapulted into the air and quickly climbed up into a cloud bank. In the distance we saw the lumbering Focke-Wulf 200 approach the convoy. Not expecting to encounter a fighter plane out in the middle of the Atlantic Ocean, the German bomber made what seemed like an almost leisurely approach, coming in low and slow, taking its time picking out its first victim. When the Focke-Wulf was still about 4 nautical miles away, the Hurricane darted out of the cloud cover and pounced.

The German gunners were caught completely off guard as the Hurricane poured rounds from its eight machine guns into one of the Focke-Wulf's engines for a good four seconds before there was any return fire.

The bomber banked sharply. The nimble Hurricane bobbed and weaved to avoid the German gunners' defensive fire, all the while firing off bursts from its machine guns each time there was an opening. Smoke began to pour out of one of the Fw 200's engines. Then flames began to lick down from the engine cowling toward the back of the wing.

The Hurricane pilot must have guessed what was about to happen next, because he banked away sharply just as the Fw 200 exploded in a huge fireball half a mile above the waves. No parachutes appeared, and the flaming wreckage fell like a load of scrap metal straight into the ocean.

For the Hurricane pilot, though, the drama wasn't over yet. None of our ships had a flight deck for him to make a return landing on. We watched as the Hurricane looped around behind the convoy, coming up from the rear, all the while intentionally losing speed and altitude. When he was a couple thousand feet ahead of the lead ship, he slid the canopy back, rolled the Hurricane upside down and dropped straight out. The Hurricane continued flying on its own for a few seconds until, pilotless, it began to nose in toward the water, hitting the waves and tearing itself to pieces. Meanwhile the pilot's parachute opened and our lead ship made straight for him.

The pilot splashed down into the water, his parachute landing on top of him. Then I couldn't see anything else because the lead ship was blocking my view.

The motor launch had arrived on the scene less than two minutes after the British pilot hit the water, but we found out afterward that it was too late. Buffetted by the waves, the pilot had been caught in his parachute lines and pulled under. He drowned before the motor launch crew could free him. He had shot down the German bomber and prevented it from sinking our ships and killing who knows how many sailors. But he lost his own life in the process. Clearly, the CAM ships were a desperate stopgap measure.

Then the Allies began to patrol the shipping lanes with a few small escort carriers. They only held a handful of planes each, but unlike on the CAM ships, the planes could take off and return safely after their missions. The escort carriers were spread very thinly throughout the North Atlantic, not nearly enough to fully cover the route, and their single-engine aircraft carried only a handful of depth charges. We still lacked proper cover from the heavy, land-based bombers whose massive loads of depth charges terrified the U-boats so much that they submerged on sight. But the presence of even a small number of fighters helped keep the Fw 200s away, and those fighters and the light bombers could spot submerged U-boats and lead our destroyers and corvettes to their targets.

* * *

For the next several months we began to breathe a sigh of relief as the convoys we escorted across the Atlantic got through unscathed, other than a few submarine scares here and there.

Soon the balance tipped again though, because now the Germans were building more U-boats than ever. Despite our best efforts we lost more than a hundred ships per month during the fall of 1942.

Then we caught a break in January and February of 1943. Things were going well for our side all around. The Russians finally defeated the Germans at Stalingrad, a long, brutal battle that had gone on for months. The convoys we'd escorted had carried a lot of the supplies on the first leg of the journey to Russia's Red Army, so it was a relief to hear that it was having an effect. In North Africa as well, the Allied armies were pushing back Rommel's famed Afrika Korps. All that combat meant that more supplies than ever were needed.

On the North Atlantic, things were going our way too. The recent winter storms had been so vicious that they kept the U-boats out of action much of the time. Once again we were chipping ice and frozen puke off our ships with every spare second we had, but at least we didn't have to worry about getting blown to bits by Nazi submarines. During one of those storms, so much sea water poured into our mess deck that every last item in our storage lockers was soaked. I came off watch to find my spare uniform, my pens, notebooks, all of Aileen's letters — everything I had that wasn't on my back — floating in grimy salt water. All the ink had bled and I couldn't make out a single word of the letters. The only consolation was that when I got to Greenock, I would see Aileen and have a couple of weeks' reprieve from it all. And she would write me new letters to replace the ones that had been obliterated by the sea water.

Chapter Eleven
February 1943

As soon as we arrived in port I took the train to Glasgow, then walked from the station through the side streets toward Bell Lane. As I recognized familiar streets near Aileen's house, I found myself walking faster. No matter how bad a crossing had been, I could always count on having a good time and feeling like myself again once I was with Aileen. I passed the intersection where Ken and I had always parted ways, then headed up the street and rounded the corner to Bell Lane. For a moment I thought I'd made a wrong turn. The scene in front of me was partly familiar . . . but partly made no sense at all. I stopped and stared, unable to understand what I was seeing.

In the middle of Bell Lane was a gaping crater. I was confused. I checked the metal street sign affixed to the brick row house on the corner beside me. It read *Bell Lane,* all right. But some of the houses that were supposed to be there were missing. Then I felt panicky. I ran down the street, counting off the house numbers as I went. They stopped at 33 and didn't resume until 41, on the other side of the roped off, rubble-strewn area. There was no 37 Bell Lane. No door, no door knocker. Just a crater filled with bricks, timber and other debris. That couldn't be possible, I told myself. It didn't make any sense.

It was the middle of the afternoon and there was no one else out on the quiet street. I pounded on a few doors, but nobody answered. I began running, retracing my steps, searching my memory for some recollection of a police station or a fire station. Before I'd reached the end of the block, an old, white-haired man emerged from his house with a small terrier on the end of a leash. I pointed toward the crater, trying to form words that would not come out. He furrowed his brow as he looked at me.

"What happened there?" I blurted out.

The old man sighed. "German air raid."

I couldn't catch my breath. My heart was racing. I already knew what he was going to say, but I kept wishing that somehow it would turn out differently, so I listened carefully to his explanation.

"The Germans were bombing Greenock," he said. "One of their planes was damaged by our anti-aircraft fire and dumped its bombs prematurely — to lighten its load and make it back to base, I suppose. Those homes took a direct hit from one of the five-hundred-pound bombs. None of us were in the air raid shelters because we weren't the ones under attack. The plane just happened to be flying overhead. It was a terrible explosion. Even though my house is at the other end of the street, it felt like the roof was coming down on me. Blew out all the windows."

It was then I noticed that he had a number of small cuts on his face and hands from where the broken glass had hit him.

I could picture the scene because it was so much like what had happened when I'd shot the bomber with my Oerlikon. This German plane hadn't even targeted the houses; it was just a horrible chance occurrence.

My mind raced, trying to imagine some way that the outcome could have been less catastrophic than it appeared to be. Maybe Aileen was working at the munitions factory when it happened. Maybe her father was at work too. Her mother could have been out shopping, and Jimmy at school.

"What happened to the people who lived here?" I asked.

He shook his head. His expression was grim. "No survivors. None from any of the homes that were hit directly." His face softened. "Did you know any of them?"

Just the question alone, his use of the past tense *did* instead of the present *do*, was enough to make me feel like I was sinking in quicksand with the world collapsing in on top of me. "Yes. The Hendersons," I managed. "Aileen. Her brother Jimmy. Her parents."

The old man looked at me sadly. "I'm sorry, son," he began. "Didn't know them well. They seemed like nice people."

I looked back toward the crater.

"Would you like to have a cup of tea?" he asked.

"Thank you, no," I replied.

I felt dizzy, like the earth was opening up beneath me and swallowing me whole along with those houses. I staggered away. The man tried to talk to me, but I had this strange sensation, like I was outside of my own body. All I could hear was my blood pounding in my head.

I walked and walked and walked until I had calmed down enough to find a police station, where I related the details. The police only confirmed what the old man had told me. There were no survivors. The funerals had been three weeks ago.

I tried to picture where I would have been at that

time on that particular day, anything to somehow make it all connect. But it didn't. I couldn't believe this was really happening. I would never see Aileen's grin ever again, never gaze into her brown eyes, smell her perfume or see her glide around the dance floor, feel the warmth of her body against mine, or her kiss on my lips. I would never see Jimmy, that gap-toothed little boy with the red hair, or the pleasant couple who had been so kind to me after the harrowing experience of my first major convoy battle.

It just didn't seem possible. But of course I knew it was. It was *very* possible. By now I had seen dozens of people get killed. They had probably all had loved ones too, so why should I or Aileen be any different from anybody else?

I didn't know what to do with myself alone in Glasgow, so I returned to barracks and asked to be reassigned to the next ship heading to Halifax.

It was an uneventful crossing in which HQ managed to divert us around all the wolf packs. I was almost disappointed. I wanted to fire a shell into a U-boat and watch it sink, or blast a German bomber out of the sky. Make some Germans pay for what they did to Aileen.

Chapter Twelve
Spring 1943

When I got back to Halifax and went ashore, the first thing I decided to do was to get away from the base and clear my head. Going to the Ajax Club was no longer an option, because the hoity-toity, holier-than-thou crowd in Halifax had pressured the city into shutting it down ages ago.

As I walked to the gates I ran into Fontaine, my shipmate from my first voyage across. I asked him if he wanted to go with me to see a movie.

"Sounds good, but I'm on duty in two hours," he answered. "Maybe tomorrow?"

"Sure thing," I replied.

Then I left the base and walked toward the one theatre in the entire city. When I arrived there was already a lineup around the block, and an usher said there was no more room. Since there was nothing else to do, I went for a walk instead, just trying to distract myself, really, from thinking about what had happened to Aileen.

I hadn't gone very far before I saw that Halifax had taken on the appearance of a prison camp.

There seemed to be shore patrol everywhere, hanging out on every street corner and in front of every restaurant, pestering sailors for ID papers. It didn't make any sense. We were locked in a life-and-death struggle with Hitler's U-boats, and meanwhile, here were these guys who never took a step off dry land, bossing us and throwing their weight around, but basically contributing zilch to the war effort.

On Gottingen Street a couple of them asked to see my papers. I showed my ID without comment and went on my way. Two blocks later I was stopped again by a couple more shore patrol. Then it happened again on Cornwallis Street. These guys not only asked to see my pass, but asked where I was going and why. We were literally within sight of the last patrol, and I was sure that they must have seen me show my ID already.

"What's the matter — slow day?" I asked. "I've already shown my pass twice, including to those guys on the corner."

"Well, you can show it to us too, wise guy," cracked one of them.

"In case you haven't noticed, there's a *war* on," I said. "Can't you find something more useful to do with yourselves than bugging the guys who are doing the fighting?"

His lip curled. "That's enough smart talk out of you!" he growled. Then he gave me a shove.

I hadn't done anything wrong, and I hadn't laid a hand on them. But I didn't feel like being pushed around by some idiot with an attitude. So I pushed him right back. His partner came at me and I gave him a shove too. The rest was predictable. They arrested me and marched me down to the base.

The captain wasn't terribly pleased at the news. "Listen, O'Connell, I know the shore patrol are a bunch of clowns, but why the hell did you have to hit them?" he asked.

"Sir, I never hit them," I replied. "They shoved me, so I shoved them back. That's all. If I'd hit them, they'd both be in the hospital right now."

He sighed. "You know I can't just let this go," he said, "even if I wanted to. The brass hats will be all over me if I don't throw them a bone."

"Yes, sir, I suppose," I replied.

I was given two weeks in the brig. It was near-solitary confinement in a room with no paper, no pens or pencils. It might seem easier than being thrown about in a hammock in a stinking mess deck, or up in a crow's nest inhaling bunker fuel exhaust and looking for German submarines intent on blasting you to kingdom come. But the last thing I wanted was to be alone with my thoughts. I kept thinking about Aileen, her brother, her mom and her dad. I thought about the sailor who died alone on the mess table beneath my hammock. I even thought about the German gunner in the plane, and wondered if I'd killed him, or sent him home crippled for the rest of his life.

After ten days, I heard a key in the door. A shore patrolman stuck his head into my cell. "You're in luck. Things have gone to hell out there. They need your useless butt out on convoy duty more than we need it in here."

I was given orders to return to my ship immediately. When I got there, I found out that the battle had taken a dramatic turn against us.

One of the guys on my first watch, a fellow by the name of Lougee, had just been transferred to the ship after coming in off a westbound convoy.

"It's a mess out there. Word is that the Krauts have broken our codes. On the last trip over, HQ had us changing directions all the time. But no matter which way they directed us, the wolf packs were there, waiting for us."

This was frightening news. In late 1942 we'd been losing about a hundred merchant ships per month, which was already a terrifying figure. Then, in just one four-day period during March, we had lost twenty-two merchant ships. We all knew we couldn't take those kinds of losses for long. Now the Germans were sinking our freighters faster than we could build them. The rumour was that Britain's oil and gasoline stockpiles had hit an all-time low, with only enough for three more months. If the situation didn't improve in a hurry, we would lose the war. Even the normally stoic Churchill was reportedly so alarmed that he was considering cancelling the convoys altogether, except that nobody could think of an alternative. It was the worst crisis we had faced so far in the entire war.

The mood was grim as we sailed into the frigid waters of a late-winter Atlantic to shepherd our convoy across. Two convoys that had sailed ahead of ours had been torn apart by huge wolf packs made up of dozens of submarines. We had every expectation of meeting a similar fate. But then, just as suddenly, the tables turned once again.

While out in the middle of the Black Pit, I was happily surprised to see, for the first time, an Allied B-24 Liberator bomber. An aircraft with exceptionally long range, the Liberator had been monopolized by the Royal Air Force and the United States Army Air Force for bombing missions over continental Europe. But rumour was that Churchill himself had personally ordered them to be transferred to Coastal Command because of the dire situation out here in the North Atlantic. So they were at last assigned in force to convoy escort duty. The B-24s operated from bases in Newfoundland, Iceland and Great Britain, so now, no matter how far out in the Atlantic we were, we'd see them on air patrol, and we'd hear about them attacking and sinking U-boats where the German subs used to roam freely.

The escort carriers were starting to give the Germans some grief as well. On one particular day in May, I was just coming on watch when the action stations alarm sounded. The cox'n said that a Grumman Avenger patrol plane from an escort group ahead of ours had caught a German U-boat unawares on the surface, 6 miles ahead. The plane had unloaded all four of its depth charges on the sub. The radio operator said that three went wide but the fourth had come down close enough to do some damage before the U-boat escaped by crash-diving. The plane crew had observed a small oil slick on the water afterward, but no debris. That meant the sub was still hiding down there somewhere, waiting for its chance to escape. We were the closest surface vessel, so it was up to us to finish them off before they could do that.

"Full speed ahead!" I heard the captain shout from the bridge.

"Aye-aye!" came the response.

An instant later the thrum of the engines vibrated through the soles of my boots. Black smoke belched from our stacks as the stokers gave it everything the *Wildrose* had to try to close the gap between us and the sub.

From my gun position I spotted the American plane circling above the spot where the U-boat had dived. As we closed in, the Avenger made a final circuit over the oil slick. Then, probably out of ammunition and low on fuel, it headed back toward its carrier, flying past us so close we could see the crew's faces in the cockpit. We waved and cheered. The plane waggled its wings, then banked away, disappearing into a grey cloud bank.

Now it was just us and the U-boat. We knew that German subs could travel up to 7 nautical miles an hour underwater. So in the twenty minutes or so since it had submerged, the sub could be anywhere within about 17 square nautical miles. And that area would only get bigger the longer it took us to find them.

We began tracing a grid pattern over the water, with the sub's last known position at its centre. Our ASDIC operators listened for any telltale *pings*.

Except for the faint thrumming of the engines below, and the sound of the bow spray as the *Wildrose* plowed through the waves, everything was strangely silent. Nobody spoke. Then I heard a shout relayed from the ASDIC room.

"Contact!"

They had picked up the unmistakeable *ping* of a submarine. My heart felt like it was jumping into my throat. We were going into combat.

We had recently been refitted with a new weapon, something called Hedgehog. A lot of the fellows weren't very enthusiastic about it. The usual way to attack a sub was to drop depth charges after you'd passed over it. But Hedgehog was a new system using mortars that were fired forward through the air and into the water 200 yards ahead of our bow.

We were told that Hedgehog would be a big improvement over depth charges. Depth charges always went off when they reached their assigned depth, whether they were near a submarine or not. They made a huge explosion that, while satisfying for the crew to see, often did little or no damage to a lurking submarine, but caused such a disturbance in the water that the ASDIC operators lost contact with the sub, often allowing it to escape. Hedgehog mortars detonated *only* if they struck a submarine, so the ASDIC operators never lost contact with their target, and could keep tracking a sub if the mortars missed it. That would give us a major advantage fighting the U-boats. Or so we had been told. A lot of the sailors were very skeptical.

The captain gave the order and a shower of mortars shot like rockets off our deck and landed in a *V* pattern far ahead of our bow, diving straight down, nose-first. Everything was quiet again, except for the wind and the waves and the *thrum* of our engines. The Hedgehog charges sank at a rate of 23 feet per second, and no U-boat operated below about 650 feet — usually less than half that depth. So after thirty seconds, I knew it was a miss.

The ASDIC operators maintained contact with the sub and we turned sharply, getting into position to fire once more. With another loud *crack* a second salvo flew over us and splashed into the water 100 yards or so off our bow. I counted to thirty again. Nothing. Some of the guys shook their heads.

"Another genius move by the brass," muttered a sailor. "I don't know why we didn't stick to depth charges."

An explosion — even an ineffective one that

made it harder to track a submarine — at least made us feel like we were doing something.

The ship leaned hard as the wheelman turned tightly to get us into attack position once more. When we straightened out of our turn, the captain ordered a third volley. The mortars arced through the air once again and nose-dived into the waves. By the time I had counted to fifteen I was beginning to think that the U-boat had escaped, leaving us to eat our rotten meat, scrape our frozen puke off our ships and wonder where they were going to strike next. But then there was a low rumble that I felt as much as heard. Water boiled up out of the ocean ahead.

"It's a hit!" came a shout from the ASDIC hut.

Everyone cheered.

The only question was how much damage we'd done. Depending on the answer to that, the sub was either going straight to the bottom or straight to the top, which could be dangerous. Even a stricken U-boat was armed to the teeth with deck guns and was easily able to fight it out with a single corvette.

A huge air bubble broke on the surface. That meant we'd cracked open their ballast chambers, so they wouldn't be able to dive. A heavy oil slick rose a few seconds later. The acrid smell of diesel oil reached my nostrils. We had shattered their fuel tanks. They were seriously wounded.

"She's coming up!" shouted the ASDIC operator.

"Ready with the deck guns!" a petty officer ordered.

I made one last check of my Oerlikon. A few seconds later the sub's dark grey bow erupted out of the waves on a steep angle. It looked ugly and evil, like the nose of a massive, primordial shark rising up out of the depths. Then the conning tower appeared. Painted on the side of it was an image of a trident-wielding Neptune, his face a grinning skeleton. These guys wanted to make an impression, that was for sure. When the submarine settled, it was low in the water and listing to port. The conning tower hatch opened and several officers appeared.

One of our crew, a fellow by the name of Schumacher, spoke some German. He raised a megaphone to his lips and called out to them to surrender. I didn't know any German, but from the intensity of Schumacher's voice, anybody would have known he wasn't fooling around. The submarine crew gave their response a moment later, not by raising their hands or waving a white flag, but by racing for their deck guns. The sub sat low in the water compared to us, and was so close that the crew on our 4-inch gun couldn't lower it enough to get a shot off.

"Fire at will," an officer called out.

The German crew were pulling the watertight plugs out of the barrels of their deck guns when I opened up on them with the Oerlikon. It was one thing to fire at a machine, like an airplane or a submarine, but shooting at living, breathing humans was the most difficult thing I'd ever done. But it was clear that they were hell-bent on firing at us, so I sprayed their deck with automatic cannon fire. As my shells raked the submarine, I saw German sailors falling into the water. I didn't know if they were dead, or jumping over the side to save their lives, and I didn't have time to think about it.

Meanwhile, as we closed the gap, several other men had now emerged from the sub, standing in the conning tower, firing sub-machine guns at us as cover so that their comrades could get to the deck guns. I aimed my Oerlikon on the conning tower and the guys with the machine guns. My shells slammed into the tower, making so much smoke as they exploded that within a few seconds I could barely see my target. There was now no more return fire from the U-boat.

I stopped firing a moment later to let the smoke clear. The sub's conning tower was so full of holes it looked like a salt shaker. Bodies of German submariners lay inside the tower and others slumped over the edge. One of them had most of his head missing. Even then the sub kept going, the remaining crew hoping to somehow outrun us on the surface.

Since we were too close to use our big gun, the captain ordered a ramming attack. The engines roared and the water churned behind us as we quickly built up speed, heading straight for the sub, which was damaged so it couldn't outrun us. The cox'n, an old-timer in his forties, had taken part in a ramming attack during the First World War. He turned and shouted to us, "Get down, and hang onto your hats, boys! When we hit that eel, there's going to be a hell of a thump, and you don't want to get thrown into the drink with all those Krauts!"

I was already strapped into my seat on the Oerlikon, but I put my hands against my gun shield and braced myself. A second later there was a bone-rattling crash of metal on metal. It felt like we'd run into a wall.

When I looked over the railing, there was no more gun or gun deck on the German submarine. Its hull had been crushed and it was sinking fast now. Most of the crew were dead, either shot or drowned, but some managed to escape from inside the hull as it sank. They came to the surface, waving their hands in surrender.

Because they were an elite branch of Germany's military, U-boat crews didn't have uniforms or dress codes like everybody else. With their long hair, beards, denim shirts and leather jackets, they looked more like thugs than the crew of a military vessel. We lowered the scramble nets. Some of the submariners were too badly injured to hold on to the nets, so the captain lowered the lifeboat and a few of us went down and pulled the remaining survivors out of the water. The last one I picked up was covered in so much oil that all I could see were the whites of his eyes and the pink of his mouth when he shouted for help.

I grabbed onto his arms and started to pull him into the boat, but he was so oily that I lost my grip and he slipped back into the sea. A large wave hit us and he disappeared under the surface. A few seconds later I saw the whites of his eyes emerge again. He looked terrified and desperate, gasping for air. Another wave broke over him and in an instant he was gone. Simple as that.

I had been so angry at the Germans for what they'd done that all I could think of was shooting down one of their planes or blasting one of their subs. But now, seeing this guy scared out of his wits and struggling for his life, I suddenly felt sorry for him. I leaned out over the side of the boat, the way George used to with the dip net when we were landing a fish. I reached down, all the way to my armpit, but all I felt was icy cold water immediately starting to numb my fingers. Then something bumped against my fingertips. I felt his shoulders, but his arms had gone limp, too slippery to get hold of. I reached down farther until my face was almost in the water. I felt his belt. I pulled as hard as I could. I almost fell over the side of the lifeboat, and with my last ounce of strength hauled him over the gunwale. He didn't move. I wasn't sure if he was even alive. I put my hands on his chest and gave it a few short, sharp jabs, the way I'd been taught. Then he coughed hard and spat up a huge mouthful of oily water.

His eyes opened. "*Danke*," he said weakly.

Of the U-boat's crew of fifty, there were only eighteen survivors. We put the prisoners down in the boiler room, in the very bottom of the ship, where we could easily stand guard over them from above. When the last of them had clambered down the stairs into the room, Schumacher stood by the hatch above them and gestured to his rifle. With his limited German and his .303, he made it abundantly clear to the survivors that if any of them tried to make a break for it, harmed any of our crew or tried to sabotage the ship, they'd be shot without a moment's hesitation. The U-boat crew didn't make any trouble for us after that.

Our battle that day seemed to be the start of an overall pattern. After almost losing everything, we had come back from the brink. The Allies' combination of new weapons and tactics was suddenly turning the tide in our favour. The Hedgehog was killing subs far more efficiently than the depth charges, and our aircraft had a new secret weapon, an air-launched torpedo that could chase a submerged sub and home in on the sound of its engines. The combined effect on the U-boats was devastating. After savaging our convoys earlier in the year, the Germans were getting it handed back to them in spades. They lost sixteen U-boats in March, another sixteen in April, and then in May a staggering forty-two. After losing almost a quarter of their operational submarines in one month, the German Navy was forced to withdraw its fleet from the North Atlantic.

Chapter Thirteen
Summer 1943–Spring 1945

With the U-boats now driven from our shipping lanes, the build-up to the rumoured invasion of Europe began. Tanks, artillery, guns, fuel, ammunition all poured into Britain in the merchant ships we escorted. We knew that Germany's Admiral Doenitz still had a huge submarine fleet at his disposal, and we guessed he was holding it in reserve for a decisive moment. We all figured that moment would come whenever we launched the cross-Channel invasion into France. So our job now became to hunt and kill the U-boats in European waters.

Because of my gunnery experience I was taken off corvette duty and assigned to the destroyer HMCS *Mohawk*. I had come to appreciate the *Wildrose*, but I didn't have an instant of remorse when I was transferred off it. I was excited as I stepped up the gangplank onto the *Mohawk*. Comparing it to the *Wildrose* was like comparing a thoroughbred racehorse to a mule. They were two different creatures altogether.

More than twice as fast as a corvette, the *Mohawk* had six 4.7-inch guns to the *Wildrose*'s single 4-inch gun. In addition, it had six of the new 40-millimetre guns, a weapon that could fire 2-pound explosive shells almost as fast as a machine gun. It was much better suited to doing battle close to the heavily defended European mainland.

Once aboard, I was happy to discover that Ken was part of the crew. We worked different gun stations now, but when we were off watch we got to pass the time together, playing cards or talking while we sunned ourselves on the deck. For a time we were stationed off Spain and in the Mediterranean, and Ken joked about getting paid to work on his tan. And destroyers were much more watertight than corvettes, so we never got soaked when we slept. The *Mohawk* was an altogether more civilized vessel to serve on.

On August 27, 1943, we were off the coast of France when our radar picked up a formation of Luftwaffe bombers heading our way. Ken and I were at our gun positions. His station was just forward of mine. There were no Allied fighter planes in the area to drive away the bombers, but we weren't panicking. By now I had a lot of confidence in our new 40-millimetre Bofors gun. It was a devastating anti-aircraft weapon. Each one fired 120 shells a minute, and just a single well-placed round could take out a German plane.

The Luftwaffe bombers soon appeared on the horizon — twin-engine Dornier 217s. Our long-range 4.7-inch guns opened up on them. That seemed to be having the intended effect, because the bombers kept their distance to avoid the flak bursts, and one even dropped its bomb toward the open ocean. I thought that meant the plane had been hit by our flak, and was lightening its load. But then I noticed something odd. Instead of falling into the water, the "bomb" that the plane had dropped kept coming our way. As it got closer I could see that it had stubby wings and some kind of rocket engine emitting a plume of smoke. It was closing fast — I guessed around 600 miles an hour, three times faster than a German bomber.

When it got within range we opened up with the Bofors guns. But it was coming in so fast I couldn't track it properly, and neither could Ken or any of the other gunners. Every shell I fired seemed to explode hundreds of feet behind it. We couldn't even swivel our guns fast enough to keep up to this thing. Then as it hurtled toward us I had a sickening realization: its trajectory was carrying it right toward Ken's gun station.

"Come on, Kenny, get it! *Get it!*" I shouted into the roar of our guns. But everything that he, I and all the other gunners fired suddenly felt maddeningly slow. Then came the moment when I realized we were really not going to get away from this thing. It fell below the level of my gun and a fraction of a second later came a roar and a deafening crash like nothing I've ever experienced before.

The world went black.

When I regained consciousness, there was smoke everywhere. The emergency klaxon alarm was ringing. I got to my knees, grabbed onto my gun and hauled myself to my feet. My head was pounding and I felt weak and nauseated. I peered out cautiously from behind my gun position and saw that Ken's gun turret was completely gone. Then I looked down and saw that I was totally covered in blood and bits of flesh and guts. I thought I'd been wounded, but I couldn't feel any bleeding anywhere. I realized I didn't have a scratch. Beside me was part of a body. There was nothing left of it from the waist up. I could see feet, legs and a belt around the top of the trousers. But above that there was nothing, just a piece of a spinal column sticking out. Then I realized what I was looking at. Ken . . . The gore that was covering me was *Ken*.

The dizziness became overwhelming and I

started to black out. I fell to my knees and vomited into the blood and the debris. Then I passed out.

When I came to, I was in the sick bay.

I looked down at myself and saw that they'd stripped my uniform off, washed the blood and gore off me and put me into clean underwear and a T-shirt.

"You've had a severe concussion," said a medic. "But you're lucky to be alive. I'm sorry about your friend. Five other guys on the gun crew died too."

They buried Ken's remains at sea that same afternoon, along with the bodies of the other victims. I awoke in the night, still in the sick bay, sweating and throwing up from the concussion. They had given me some kind of painkiller and I couldn't tell if I was asleep or awake half the time. Strange images and thoughts drifted into my mind. As I slipped in and out of consciousness, I had a memory of the day that I'd told Ken the answers to the aircraft identification test in Scotland. I knew if I hadn't done that, he would have washed out and been assigned to some other duty. Maybe then he'd still be alive. Or maybe he just would have been killed sooner. I couldn't stop thinking about it.

Then I slipped into the dark of unconsciousness again.

* * *

When we got back to port, they put me in hospital for observation. Once the doctors were sure that I was okay, the brass sent me on leave, then reassigned me to training duty, because they figured I needed a break. I found myself back in Halifax once again, training recruits who had shown an aptitude for gunnery.

But as spring of 1944 came, I was restless. In one of her letters, my mom mentioned that Jack Byers was in Italy, fighting the Germans in the invasion that had started there the previous September. The Germans were putting up ferocious resistance, but Jack and the rest of them were gradually pushing them back and were now closing in on Rome. We knew an invasion of Western Europe was coming too. We all knew it. We didn't know exactly where or when it would happen, but everybody talked about it.

In April I requested a combat posting and was given one, on a fast, very powerful Tribal class destroyer. On the evening of June 5, 1944, we were sent out into the English Channel. It was only when we were approaching the battle zone that we were told what was happening. The Allies had just launched the biggest sea invasion in history, and it was our job to make sure that no German submarines got anywhere near our troop ships and landing craft.

As the dawn sky began to lighten over the horizon shortly after 0500 hours, I could make out the dark forms of hundreds of ships heading east. The Allied air forces appeared overhead to make sure that the sky was clear of German bombers, while down below we were on full alert to hunt U-boats. The Navy did such a good job of it that not a single German sub managed to break through our protective screen during the invasion.

The Allied landing we took part in was called D-Day. Thousands and thousands of Allied troops poured onto the shores of Normandy, and soon had established a solid beachhead and had begun driving the Nazis inland. Over the coming months, we heard about the big land battles going on, first in France, then the Low Countries and finally Germany itself. We heard reports from the Eastern Front too, where the Russians were pounding the once-mighty German army into submission and forcing them back toward Berlin. Our soldiers in Italy were driving the Germans farther and farther north. The Nazi empire was crumbling.

That didn't mean that the world was becoming any less dangerous. Just a few weeks after the

D-Day landing, I got a letter from my mom. It started off like always, saying that she hoped I was well. But then she wrote, *Billy, I've got some news to tell you, and I'm afraid it isn't good. It's about your friend Jack Byers.* I didn't have to read any further to know what she was going to tell me. Not with everything that was going on all around me. But I continued reading. *Apparently he was in a tank that was part of the advance on Rome. It hit a mine that the Germans had buried in a field. They say he died instantly.*

I had that familiar, sad sinking feeling that I was starting to get too used to. But it only increased my determination to finish this thing. And it made Hitler and the Nazis seem crazier than ever to me — insane really. Because despite the iron noose tightening around them, the Nazis seemed determined not to surrender without laying waste to Europe. With Allied troops now pushing in on them from all directions, they began firing V-1 flying bombs at England. Each carried a couple thousand pounds of explosives. Allied fighters were just fast enough to catch them, but the Nazis sent them over by the thousands, so despite the success of the Allied defences, it wasn't possible to stop all the V-1s. The killing was temporarily halted when Allied troops overran the German launch sites in Europe, by which time the V-1s had killed more than six thousand people.

I took some satisfaction knowing that we had safely shepherded a lot of the aircraft fuel, food, equipment and weapons that our troops had used in their successful campaign to put those launch sites out of action and keep driving the Nazis all the way back to Berlin.

Even then though, the Nazis weren't finished with their pointless destruction. We began hearing about mysterious explosions in London. At first the government said they were gas main ruptures, but in November Winston Churchill admitted that the British capital had been under attack by a new weapon, the V-2 ballistic missile, which flew so fast — several times the speed of sound — that there was literally no defence against it except to stop it at its source. So again we were kept busy protecting the precious cargoes of materiel that our troops needed to press home the attack and put Hitler out of business once and for all.

* * *

Over the fall and winter of 1944 and into 1945, our convoy escort work continued as busily as always. Our armies in Europe had an insatiable need for tanks, guns, equipment and supplies. All those civilians in Great Britain still needed to be fed too. We continued to encounter German subs and patrol planes, but they grew fewer and fewer, and their crews seemed to have less will to fight.

Allied scientists developed ways to jam the radio-control frequencies of the flying bombs like the one that tore through the *Mohawk*, so they became less of a threat. But we had seen first-hand that when it came to killing people, the Nazis had a particular talent for technical innovation. We never let down our guard. Even as 1945 began, it felt like a race against time to defeat them in case they had something new and even more deadly up their sleeve.

Chapter Fourteen
Spring 1945

On May 2, 1945, I was in the barracks in Halifax when I heard a CBC radio broadcast describing a link-up between Soviet and American troops on German soil, and Hitler's rumoured death. But still the German forces refused to surrender, and shortly afterward we learned that Admiral Doenitz, who had spearheaded the U-boat campaign for most of the war, had taken over from Hitler. So we got our orders to escort another supply convoy that was forming up in Halifax Harbour.

Five days later we were less than 20 nautical miles from port, preparing to join the convoy that was now about to set sail. It was almost the exact spot where only three weeks earlier a U-boat had sunk our minesweeper HMCS *Esquimalt*, killing forty-four men. I was checking my Bofors gun when I heard somebody whoop in the radio room.

"The war is over!" someone shouted. "Doenitz has surrendered."

"We've finally beaten the bastards!" shouted someone else.

A cheer went up all over the ship. We hugged each other and threw our caps in the air. We had a tot of rum to celebrate. But we couldn't be sure that all the U-boats had received the order to stand down, so even though we were ordered back to port, we stood ready to fight until we had entered Halifax Harbour and passed Georges Island.

When we docked, instead of jubilation I could feel tension in the air. A lot of sailors were resentful of the way they had been treated by the locals, and had let it be known that when the war was over there would be a "day of reckoning" for Halifax. Rear Admiral Murray, who was commander-in-chief, thought it was just talk. He gave his sailors shore leave to enjoy their victory, won at such a high cost in sweat, blood and toil, with instructions to celebrate in a "reasonable manner."

But as always, the authorities in Halifax made the wrong move. Instead of letting the sailors blow off steam and enjoy the victory they'd paid such a high price for, they closed the bars, restaurants, beer and liquor stores. Guys were roaming the streets with nowhere to go and nothing to do. The result was predictable: locals and sailors alike looted the beer and liquor stores and got drunk. A two-day orgy of looting and vandalism broke out.

I was still on active duty, so I didn't take part in any of it. From the dockyard where our ship was anchored I could hear windows smashing and the roar of the mob. As night fell it seemed like the violence might spill over into the dockyard. My captain put me on sentry duty. He pulled out a Colt .45 pistol, removed the ammo clip, then handed the gun to me.

"Stand at the top of the gangplank," he said, "And if any drunks come along looking to start trouble, you make sure they see that Colt forty-five."

"Yes, sir," I said, and took up my position.

I stood at the top of the gangplank, looking as tough and dangerous as I could, but nobody came around looking for trouble. By 2300 hours that night, things settled down. The drunks had tired themselves out, the city and the sailors all went to bed to sleep it off. And for me, the Battle of the Atlantic was over.

Epilogue

The war didn't end when we beat the Nazis. Even after Hitler committed suicide and Germany surrendered, their ally Japan stubbornly refused to capitulate, though the Japanese seemed to have little chance of winning. Japan had a serious fuel shortage, had lost most of its ships and aircraft by then and possessed very few seasoned crew to man what little it had left. On top of that, now the Japanese would have the full weight of the Allies thrown at them. But just like with Hitler, Japan's leaders didn't seem to care how many of their soldiers or civilians were killed.

After Victory in Europe (V-E) day, the Pacific War was considered a bit of a sideshow in Canada, and the RCN soon began to discharge sailors. Only those who had volunteered for Pacific service were asked to continue the fight against the Japanese. I'd heard about the things the Japanese did to our guys in Hong Kong, how they'd mistreated them, starved them and tortured them. And I'd heard about the atrocities the Japanese Imperial Army had committed in the places they conquered. This war wouldn't really be over for me until we'd given them a good drubbing and settled it once and for all. I understood how guys would want to go home after so many years in the war, but I had to finish the job. So I volunteered for the RCN's Pacific contingent.

For those of us who stayed on, all the talk was now about the Pacific War, which was shaping up to be a long and drawn-out battle to invade and occupy the Japanese mainland itself. The recent invasion of the Japanese island of Okinawa had been successful, but came at tremendous loss of life.

We suspected it would be just as rough for those of us coming late to the Pacific War. Since the Japanese were running out of trained fighter pilots, fuel and aircraft, in desperation they developed "kamikaze" tactics. They gave a recruit minimal training as a pilot, then put him into an airplane loaded with bombs and ordered him to crash into an Allied warship in a suicide attack.

I knew that as an anti-aircraft gunner it would fall to me to stop the kamikazes. I was up for the task, but I had to admit that it was a daunting prospect to go up against these fanatics. I had seen newsreel footage of kamikaze attacks on American ships, and I wasn't looking forward to meeting them in battle. Seeing them reminded me of that day on the *Mohawk* when we were attacked by the guided missile and I'd lost Ken. But this was worse. You could jam a flying bomb's radio guidance system now, rendering them useless to the enemy. But there was nothing you could do to stop a living human being who was determined to crash his plane into you, except blast him out of the sky before he got to you.

On August 7 I was aboard a destroyer near Esquimalt, on a training run, when we heard the news that the United States had dropped an atomic bomb on Hiroshima, Japan. The radio announcer said it was equal to 20,000 tons of TNT. The American president, Harry Truman, insisted that unless the Japanese surrendered, more atomic bombs would follow. But the Japanese refused to lay down their arms.

On August 9 I heard that the Americans had dropped a second atomic bomb, this one on the city of Nagasaki. Six days later came an announcement over the ship's public address system that Japan had surrendered. This time, I was really going home.

* * *

I never returned to Iroquois to live. By the time the war ended, the rest of my family had followed

George and Don to Ottawa. Partly it was because the federal government had expanded so much that there were far more jobs there than in Iroquois. And partly it was because my father had had a heart attack in 1943 while I was on convoy duty. My parents hadn't told me at the time, because they didn't want me to worry. I think the years of constant anxiety about earning a living during the Depression had taken their toll on him. After that he needed regular care, and the nearest heart specialist was in Ottawa.

As for my birthplace of Iroquois, it ceased to exist not long after the war. To make way for the St. Lawrence Seaway, crews flattened nearly every building in the town — including the stone house that had been in my family since they moved to Canada from Ireland a century earlier — so that they wouldn't be navigation hazards to ships. They built a new town that kept the name Iroquois, but that's all that's left of the original town — the name.

It strikes me as a strange coincidence that so many of the people and places that were such a big part of my life are now beneath the water. My hometown, he house I lived in, the streets and fields I played in kid, the school I went to, are all gone, covered water. Ken and my other Navy comrades and the merchant sailors who died in combat are all under water too, claimed by the sea. All of my vanquished enemies — the German submariners and their U-boats — have disappeared into the sea. The sea even took Aileen's letters away from me, washed her words right off the pages, as though she had never thought them, never written them.

It's like none of it ever happened. Except that I know it happened. Because I remember it all. And because we are free.

Historical Note

When the war began, Canada's Navy, like its Army and Air Force, was small, understaffed and ill-equipped for a major conflict. The Great Depression had thrown the Canadian government into a decade-long financial crisis, resulting in a slash-and-burn approach to spending that left the military services critically underfunded. Even when Adolf Hitler came to power and began talking tough while building up the German armed forces, Canada's prime minister, William Lyon Mackenzie King, at first reduced funding for the country's armed forces, until it became clear that war was very likely. Then the government hurriedly began expanding its military.

Even so, on the eve of World War II the Royal Canadian Navy's total combat forces consisted of only six destroyers and five minesweepers, along with two training vessels. Astonishingly, for a country with so many thousands of kilometres of coastline, Navy personnel totalled only 145 officers and 1674 men. To put that in perspective, it is less than half the number of personnel serving in the navy of the land-locked nation of Bolivia in 2014.

Stretched between bases on both the Atlantic and Pacific coasts, in Halifax and Victoria, that small number of ships and sailors was clearly inadequate even to protect Canada's own waters, let alone offer much support to its allies.

At the beginning of the war Canada and the other Allied nations were much more concerned about the Nazi's surface fleet of battleships and heavy cruisers than they were about German submarines. The latter were known as U-boats, after the German *U-boot*, an abbreviation for *Unterseeboot* — literally meaning "undersea boat." At first the German Navy, or Kriegsmarine, didn't take their U-boats as seriously as their surface fleet either. But following some spectacular military failures by the German Navy's surface fleet, combined with some equally spectacular successes by the submarine forces under the command of Admiral Karl Doenitz, Hitler began focusing his attention on his submarine fleet as the best way to choke off the supply of food, weapons and other supplies to Great Britain.

In 1940 when Hitler's forces steamrolled their way over France, Belgium, the Netherlands and Luxembourg in the so-called Blitzkrieg or

"Lightning War," strangling Britain's supply lines became a distinctly more likely scenario.

The fall of Western Europe was a dangerous situation for the Allies for a number of reasons. Because Germany now controlled France, Belgium, the Netherlands and Luxembourg, they now also controlled the industry and agriculture of those countries. They could appropriate defeated nations' goods and labour forces while denying those same resources to Great Britain.

Some may have viewed Britain as an "unsinkable aircraft carrier" from which the fight could be taken to the Nazis. But as unsinkable as the island might have been, lacking weapons to fight with and food to feed the soldiers and civilians, Great Britain would become an aircraft carrier with a starving population and dwindling resources, while its enemy grew stronger.

The United Kingdom had been a trading nation for hundreds of years. Its wealth had come from importing raw materials, then turning those raw materials into finished products it could sell for a good profit all over the world. Following that policy, Great Britain became so successful that its population outgrew its capacity to feed itself. In peacetime that didn't matter. Britain could simply import the food it needed. But in wartime, isolated on an island and fighting an enemy determined to blockade it, the situation became very different. The equation was simple, and seen through the lens of the early war years, it must have been frightening. Britain needed to import half a ton of food per person per year to feed itself. It also needed to import gasoline and oil to power its airplanes and tanks, and run its industries. All of it had to be brought in by ship. Knowing that, Hitler was determined to sink those merchant ships so that Britain would be starved into submission and forced to surrender.

After the Nazis had defeated France, the U-boats could be moved from ports on the Baltic Sea in Germany to bases on the French coast — close to Great Britain and the Allied shipping lanes. In one stroke the Germans had brought their submarines 800 kilometres closer to the battle zone, cutting down their travel time to the killing fields and giving the U-boats as much as two weeks more time at sea to stalk and sink merchant ships before returning to port. Things went so well for the U-boat crews that they began to refer to this as the "Happy Time." German and Italian submarines sank nearly three hundred Allied merchant vessels between June and October of 1940. That was far faster than they could be replaced. If the carnage continued at that rate, the Allied merchant fleet would be torpedoed into oblivion, and Great Britain starved into surrender.

At the beginning of the war Allied fighting ships were equipped with ASDIC, a technology developed by Great Britain more than twenty years earlier, during the First World War. ASDIC, or "sonar" as the Americans called it, was a device that searched for submarines by using acoustical *pings*, not unlike the echolocation system that bats use to track their prey as they fly through the dark. Under the ship were several hydrophones, which picked up the sound of the returning echoes. If the echo of a *ping* came back, the ASDIC operator knew there was something beneath his ship, reflecting the signal back to him. By gauging the tiny differences between when the echo reached each of the hydrophones, a good ASDIC operator could judge not only the depth of the submarine, but its course in relation to his own ship.

Once the ASDIC operator had the submarine under surveillance, he gave a constant stream of updates to the captain, who then gave orders through the chain of command to the depth-charge crew. The depth charge, developed during World War I, was the key weapon used against submarines throughout much of the Battle of the

Atlantic. Each one, looking like an oil drum, was packed with 130 kilograms of explosives. Its fuse was controlled by the amount of water pressure it detected, so the charges could be set to detonate at a particular depth. The operators would adjust the charges to explode at whatever depth the ASDIC operator believed the submarine to be. The charges could be rolled off a rack at the back of the ship, or fired from launchers. Under the right conditions it was an extremely effective way of killing submarines.

But many factors could make ASDIC inaccurate. Sometimes the equipment mistook whales and large schools of fish for submarines. Other times, as often happens in the ocean, the various layers of water under a ship were different temperatures, and that variation distorted the ASDIC signal even if contact was genuinely made with a U-boat, creating an inaccurate picture of where the submarine was lurking. Although depth charges created a massive explosion and huge columns of water that were satisfying for crews to watch, their detonation disrupted the ASDIC signals, sometimes giving enemy submarines a chance to escape if the sub wasn't fatally damaged in the first volley. It has been estimated that a depth charge had to explode within 5 metres of a submarine to sink it, and in the vastness of the ocean, landing a depth charge within 5 metres of an invisible target is extremely difficult.

But although ASDIC was effective under the right conditions, it had one major limitation: it could only detect *submerged* submarines. U-boats were slower underwater and required battery power when submerged, so they usually ran on the surface when they weren't afraid of being spotted — for example, at night when they were moving in on a target. In the early stages of the war, the Allied sailors had nothing to detect surfaced submarines with, except for their eyes. That limitation often proved deadly.

Later, Canadian warships became equipped with radar, which allowed them to detect surfaced submarines even on moonless nights or in fog. Another device that was useful for convoy duty was something known as HuffDuff, the sailors' slang for High-Frequency Direction Finder. The Allies had secretly created a web of radio signal detection stations from land bases throughout the North Atlantic region. The Germans had a powerful encryption device, known as Enigma, that for much of the war outsmarted Allied intelligence. But it made the Kriegsmarine so confident that their radio messages couldn't be decoded, it apparently didn't occur to the U-boat commanders that even if they weren't giving away the contents of their encoded orders and reports, they were giving away their positions simply by *sending* radio signals. With the Allies' multiple radio-signal detection stations all over the North Atlantic region, they could triangulate the U-boats' radio signals and with reasonable accuracy detect where German submarines were. This, for a time, allowed Allied Naval commanders to steer convoys away from the unwitting German submarines, which would lie in wait in large wolf packs, only to find the sea around them completely empty of targets, which had been re-routed far to the north or south.

The advantage shifted once again when the Germans for a time cracked the Allied codes. Then, even when Allied commanders ordered their convoys to change direction around a wolf pack, they would discover the Germans waiting for them wherever they went.

Aircraft played a major role as well. German long-range bombers — in particular the four-engine Focke-Wulf 200, known to the Allies as the Kurier — were deadly. Operating from bases in Norway and France, the Fw 200 bombers could attack Allied ships far out in the Atlantic.

The Allies tried to counter that threat with shore-based fighter planes, but the Kurier's long range initially allowed it to prey on Allied convoys that were beyond the reach of land-based Allied fighter planes.

Gradually the Allies closed the gap here too. At first the British built CAM ships, merchant vessels with one catapult-launched Hawker Hurricane fighter plane on each. When a German bomber was detected approaching a convoy, the Hurricane was catapulted into the air to shoot down the bomber before it could attack the ships or report their position to U-boats. It was a truly desperate measure, since there was no flight deck for the Hurricane pilot to make a return landing. After his single mission, he had to bail out of his plane and parachute as close to a rescue ship as possible. It was very risky, as parachuting into the frigid and rough water of the North Atlantic was an extremely dangerous undertaking in which a pilot could easily drown. A few months after this stopgap measure was adopted, the Allies built proper flight decks on several merchant ships, allowing fighter planes and light anti-submarine aircraft to operate.

By early 1942 the Germans were building three U-boats for every one that the Allies sank. The Allies were barely containing the U-boats already in service. In the first half of that year the Allies lost nearly six hundred merchant ships.

Gradually, as the Allies gained experience and made some technological improvements, they became more of a match for their German counterparts, raising the numbers of U-boats sunk. But then the Germans modified their Enigma coding machine again, and until the Allied code breakers could catch up, which happened in the final days of 1942, convoy commanders were again working almost in the dark.

In late 1942 the Germans were producing more U-boats than ever, and despite the Allies' best efforts they lost more than 100 ships per month during October, November and December of 1942. Then came a reprieve of sorts in January and February of 1943. It was partly because of the Allied code breakers' success in late December, and partly because the winter storms were particularly vicious. The waves were so towering, they kept the U-boats out of action much of the time because their torpedoes couldn't be targeted accurately in high seas.

In March 1943 the Germans once again gained the upper hand. In just one four-day period that month, the U-boats sank 21 ships. This rate of loss was completely unsustainable for the Allies.

Just as quickly as the scale had tipped in the Nazis' favour, it shifted to the Allies' advantage. B-24 Liberator bombers were at last assigned to convoy escort duty instead of being monopolized for bombing campaigns over Europe. Operated by the RCAF from bases in Newfoundland, and by Coastal Command on the other side of the Atlantic, the VLR B-24 Liberators were finally able to provide continual air cover, even in the middle of the Atlantic, attacking U-boats outright as well as acting as spotters for surface vessels. It has been argued that the Battle of the Atlantic might have been won much sooner had more Liberators been made available for convoy patrol duty instead of being used on bombing missions against ground targets over Europe.

In May of 1943 Allied ships and aircraft sank forty-two German U-boats, a record number. Admiral Doenitz's son was among the victims. The admiral was so shocked by the staggering losses, he temporarily withdrew his U-boat fleet from the North Atlantic.

Some historians say that was the end of the Battle of the Atlantic, because the German submarines never came back in the same numbers as before, and never achieved anything approaching their previous success rate.

Allied convoys increasingly sailed across the North Atlantic unscathed. But while the Battle of the Atlantic might have officially ended from an historical point of view, for two more long years, until May 7, 1945, sailors and submariners continued to die.

Allied forces had taken an immense toll on their enemy. Of the approximately forty thousand German submariners who went to sea, nearly thirty thousand never made it home, one of the highest mortality rates of any branch of any armed force in the world. But the Battle was very costly for the Allies as well: 36,200 Allied military personnel were killed, and 36,000 merchant seamen lost their lives.

Corvette HMCS Chambly *in Halifax in April 1941. The ship took part in missions, and was used for training, throughout the war.*

A flotilla of escort ships sails to Britain from Canada in 1941. The photo is taken from HMCS Chambly.

Though corvettes were very seaworthy, they were far from comfortable — getting soaked was a constant experience for the crew.

Two ASDIC operators aboard HMCS Battleford *listen intently for telltale pings that indicate the presence of a nearby submarine. American forces referred to ASDIC as sonar.*

DEMS (Defensively Equipped Merchant Ships) personnel take part in a gun drill.

A depth charge is fired from the deck of the corvette HMCS Pictou.

The corvette HMCS Chebogue *shows signs of massive damage inflicted by a torpedo from Germany's* U-1227 *submarine. Her stern was torn off and she was towed to Wales, out of commission.*

Allied sailors hoist the White Ensign over Germany's Kriegsmarine flag on captured U-boat U-190 *in St. John's, Newfoundland.*

As the war ended, German U-boat U-889 *surrenders off Shelburne, Nova Scotia. A Royal Canadian Navy crew prepares to board the submarine.*

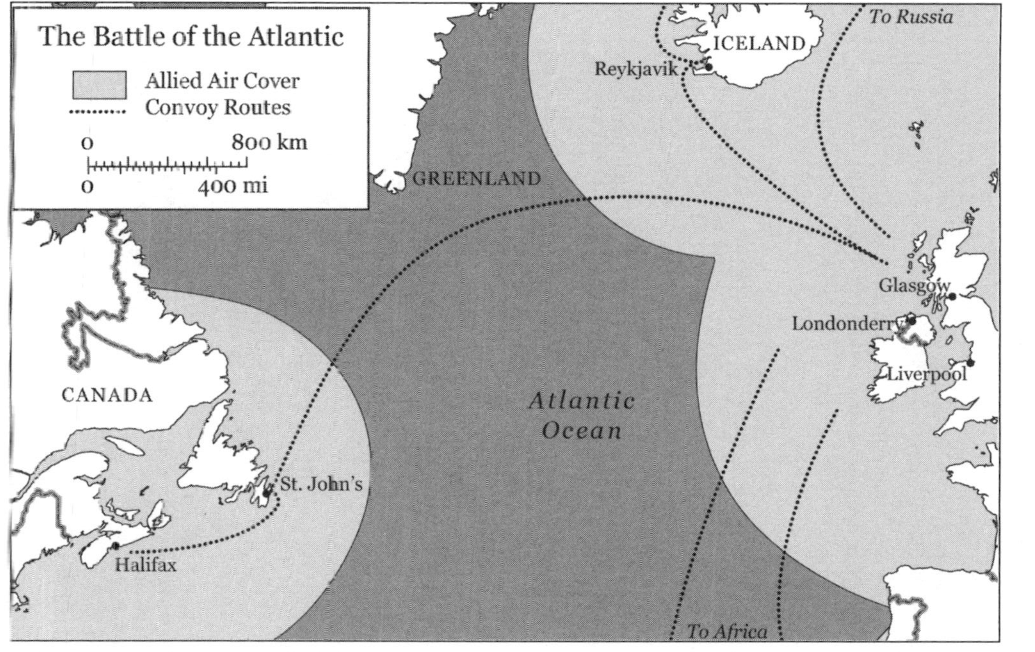

Pale grey areas indicate where Allied planes could provide cover for the convoys. The size of the mid-Atlantic Air Gap shrank as planes with longer range became available.

Credits

Cover scene (detail): *Depth charges exploding after being dropped by the destroyer HMS* VANOC..., Lt. H.W. Tomlin, Admiralty Official Collection, Imperial War Museum, A 4570.

Cover details: Andreykuzmin | Dreamstime.com; aged paper © Shustterstock/Filipchuck Oleg Vasilovich; belly band © raplett/istockphoto; (back cover) label © Shutterstock/Thomas Bethge.

Page 188: *Corvette HMCS* Chambly *in Halifax, April 1941,* Library and Archives Canada / Department of National Defence, PA-105255.
Page 189: *View from H.M.C.S.* Chambly, *the First Corvette Flotilla en route from Halifax, [N.S.], to St. John's, Newfoundland, 23 May 1941,* Library and Archives Canada / Department of National Defence fonds, PA-037447.
Page 190: *View — probably aboard H.M.C.S.* Trillium, *1943,* Library and Archives Canada / Department of National Defence fonds, PA-037474.
Page 191: *R. Cosburn and Lieutenant F.A. Beck (right) at the Asdic set on the bridge of H.M.C.S.* Battleford, *Sydney, Nova Scotia, Canada, November 1941,* Library and Archives Canada / Department of National Defence fonds, PA-184187.
Page 192: *DEMS (Defensively Equipped Merchant Ships) personnel taking part in gun drill aboard an unidentified merchant ship, Halifax, Nova Scotia, Canada, 29 November 1942,* Library and Archives Canada / Department of National Defence fonds, PA-016528.
Page 193: *Firing of a depth charge from the corvette H.M.C.S.* Pictou *at sea, March 1942,* Library and Archives Canada / Department of National Defence fonds, PA-116838.
Page 194: *Damage done to the Canadian Frigate H.M.C.S.* Chebogue *after a torpedo from a German U-Boat ripped into her port quarter, 1944,* Library and Archives Canada / Department of National Defence fonds, PA-141300.
Page 195: *Conning tower of German submarine* U-190, *showing Schnorkel mast and White Ensign flying over Kriegsmarine flag, 1945,* Library and Archives Canada / Department of National Defence fonds, PA-145577.
Page 196: *Surrender of the German submarine* U-889 *off Shelburne, Nova Scotia, Canada, 13 May 1945,* Library and Archives Canada / Department of National Defence fonds, PA-173333.
Page 197: Map by Paul Heersink/Paperglyphs.

The publisher wishes to thank Janice Weaver for her detailed checking of the factual elements, and naval historian Dr. Roger Sarty, co-author of *No Higher Purpose: The Official Operational History of the Royal Canadian Navy, Vol. II part 1: 1939–1943* and *A Blue Water Navy: The Official Operational History of the Royal Canadian Navy, Vol. II, Part 2: 1943–1945*, for his comments on the manuscript.

About the Author

Edward Kay became interested in the Battle of the Atlantic when he found a wartime newspaper article which included an interview with one of his uncles, Bob McDonald. In the article, Petty Officer McDonald was interviewed about his World War II experiences, particularly the time when his ship sank a U-boat. Three of Edward's uncles served on combat vessels of the Royal Canadian Navy during the war, but he says "they were humble and never spoke of their experiences. This article made me curious to find out more, and when I did, I knew it was a story that should be told." The story of Bill O'Connell's family in Iroquois is also partially based on Edward's own family history.

During his research for this novel, Edward interviewed a number of veterans, and got hold of an old Royal Navy training film from 1943 for orienting raw recruits about shipboard life, and one about training air crew in how to attack subs. Both were helpful in researching scenes for this book.

Edward believes that the stories of the brave sailors who escorted the convoys bringing crucial supplies to Great Britain have not been told nearly as often as stories of battles such as the D-Day landings or the campaigns across France, the Netherlands and Belgium. "The Battle of the Atlantic was critically important to the outcome of the war, and it's an under-represented story still waiting to be fully told."

He also unearthed some attitudes that he hadn't come across in other World War II references. Several veterans told him that they felt very unwelcome in Halifax whenever they were on shore — quite different from how they were regarded in Britain. They spoke of having to rent tiny rooms at high prices, hostility from some of the citizens, and having to contend with very high prices for any goods being sold near the harbour. The sailors were also not allowed to go very far from the harbour itself, so tensions were sometimes high. The shore patrol incident came from one of the veterans Edward interviewed.

One of the most intriguing things Edward discovered in his research was the fake telephone pole "guns" that the first corvettes had in place to fool German U-boat crews into thinking that they weren't virtually defenceless. Though the corvette his character Bill serves on came slightly later in the war than the first handful that sailed to England, Edward thought the telephone pole "gun" was just too good a detail to leave out.

Edward's earlier novels are *Star Academy* and *Star Academy: Dark Secrets.* He has also written for *The Globe and Mail*, *Canadian Geographic* and the CBC show *This Hour Has 22 Minutes.*

Other books in the I AM CANADA series

Prisoner of Dieppe
World War II
Hugh Brewster

Blood and Iron
Building the Railway
Paul Yee

Shot at Dawn
World War I
John Wilson

Deadly Voyage
RMS Titanic
Hugh Brewster

Behind Enemy Lines
World War II
Carol Matas

A Call to Battle
The War of 1812
Gillian Chan

Storm the Fortress
The Siege of Quebec
Maxine Trottier

Fire in the Sky
World War I
David Ward

Graves of Ice
The Lost
Franklin Expedition
John Wilson

For more information please see the I AM CANADA
website: www.scholastic.ca/iamcanada